PRAISE

"Rachel Rodman's short, punchy experiments are a beautiful tightrope act of awe, wonder, and delicate surprise. Reading each one is like a delicious little treat, one you want to savor, and then return to again for seconds when you are done."
  —Paul Jessup, author of *Daugther of the Wormwood Star*

"These are stories you can dip into whenever you need a palate cleanser from regular life."
  —Jennifer E. Hilt, author of *The Trope Thesaurus*

"Rachel Rodman is the direct literary descendant of Angela Carter & a stealthy assassin of the Brothers' Grimm."
  —Jessica Hagy, author of *One Morning*

also by Rachel Rodman

Art is Fleeting
Exotic Meats and Inedible Objects

MUTANTS *and* HYBRIDS

A COLLECTION OF EXPERIMENTAL FICTION

RACHEL RODMAN

Underland Press

MUTANTS *and* HYBRIDS

Table of Contents

The Wizard of Zo

Down the Purple Cobblestone Thoroughfare, Yhtorod shuffled, aged and frail. Beside him, sleek and fastidious, sauntered his cat, Otot.

As he trudged, Yhtorod acquired three additional companions. Each of them wanted something nearly as intensely as he did.

The first, Worceracs, had a massive skull. From the soft flesh at the top, many domes protruded: a profusion of brains, syncopatedly pulsing. Worceracs rarely spoke. Her brains were hungry for oxygen; supplying them with what they demanded required most of her attention. As she walked, she wheezed and panted.

The second, Namnit, was otherwise diseased. Her exterior was hard. But it was also warped. In three sections, just above the coordinated, freakish, over-strong action of her three hearts, the metal bulged. Every second and a half, at the systolic portion of a beat, the hearts again slammed against her interior (a triple punch), and her entire body rattled.

The third, Noil Yldrawoc, was a chihuahua. Her tiny body was seamed with scars and burns, each the memento of some bizarre act of near-suicidal boldness.

Everything was the target of Noil's competitive temper. She yapped and yapped and yapped continuously. When the other companions, cowering, declined her invitation to duel, she challenged the rocks, the trees, and the very earth. "I will defeat the sun!" she cried.

*

At the end of the Purple Cobblestone Thoroughfare, Yhtorod and his companions reached the Ruby Metropolis.

Inside, everything was red: walls, roofs, roads, and footpaths. At the Wizard's Palace, soldiers in ruby-studded uniforms welcomed them, then obligingly conveyed them—no hesitation whatsoever—down a ruby-paved corridor.

"Ladies first," Yhtorod insisted, when they reached the ante-room outside the Wizard's audience chamber. Then, as Worce-racs, Namnit and Noil entered Zo's chamber together, he sat heavily on a bench in the anteroom, Otot on his lap.

Soon Worceracs reemerged, smiling delightedly. From her head, all the excess had been trimmed away. Her breathing was healthy and slow. She had also been awarded a position on Zo's janitorial staff. Brandishing her new mop, she made experimental scrubbing motions while executing a clumsy pirouette.

Namnit emerged next. Her body had also been regularized. In her chest, a single heart beat, all but imperceptible. In her eyes was a fiendish joy.

In her arms, Namnit cradled a cleaver, the implement of her new profession. As Zo's Chief Butcher, she would secure those exotic meats that many in Zo enjoyed, but were too squeamish to prepare themselves: veal, in particular, but also unicorn livers and the bashed-in brains of baby seals.

Noil emerged last, serious and silent. She wore the costume of a novitiate, black and white. In her claws she clicked a length of beads. Soon, she would begin life in a secluded convent, deep in the countryside.

Restrained by her shyness, Noil kept her gaze fixed on her feet; what little she said, she mumbled. But her mouth was curved in a modest smile, and her eyes glowed with a perfect satisfaction.

Finally, it was Yhtorod's turn. Leaving Otot in the care of Worceracs and Noil—though not, pointedly, with the fiendish Namnit—he shuffled in slowly, leaning heavily on his cane.

The audience chamber shimmered. On its walls, rubies were arranged in elaborate swirls. On a red throne at the far end of the room sat a beautiful young woman: the Wizard. She wore a red mantle and a ruby crown. In her eyes, galaxies pulsed and stars flickered.

"Ask anything," she said, speaking directly into Yhtorod's mind.

Held by her gaze, Yhtorod remembered everything. His grim childhood under the care of an abusive stepfather, and his grim adulthood spent deep in the coal mines of West Virginia, inhaling the dust, and the grim growths that now spread slowly through his chest and pelvis, from which his doctors had provided no relief, refusing him the prescription he craved. And the tsunami, too, which had borne him to Zo, and into which he had walked directly, starting from the porch of his assisted living facility, not trying to escape. And how it had only been here, in this magical metropolis and in this land beyond the rainbow, that he had dared to hope.

"I wish to die," he said.

Jonah and Delilah

A whale? I say.

He loves me, he says, as much as any man might love a woman. But with this whale, everything is different. Everything is *more*. When he is inside her . . .

Enough.

That's fine, I tell him, holding up a hand. I would certainly never . . .

The secret, he says—had I asked?—is his hair, which has never been cut. Through each strand, a peculiar strength flows, which permits him to breathe as well as she does and to swim as deeply. Because the growth of his hair has never been checked, it is also possible for him to *love* her. To be inside her for *days* at a time . . .

Enough.

He is kind, I tell him, given all this, to visit me so often.

He nods absently. He smiles. At the same time, his eyes drift away, to the view through my window.

The sea.

Me, I say—a little louder—who is merely a land creature.

What? he says.

A LAND CREATURE, I say, and feel my eyes fill.

Salt.

Water.

Tenderly, he leans over. Tenderly, he wipes my face.

He tells me that I am very beautiful. That, for a woman, I am very . . .

Then he shares his seed with me. Another kindness. It is always deep, his sharing. It is deep again this time. But I want him to be deeper. For days; *that* deep. So deep that he might never . . .

I entwine my fingers in his hair: long hair, which I have long admired, without, before this evening, entirely understanding why. As I do, I try to bring him deeper. For days: deep, deep, deep. So that he might never . . .

When he withdraws from me (it has not been days; it has not even been an hour), I let go of him. Of his hair.

Outside, it is beginning to be dark.

He kisses me again. Then he closes his eyes, half turning toward the window, where the sea is now just barely visible. I listen to him sigh, again and again; I watch as his eyes begin to flick beneath his lids.

I know exactly what he is dreaming of.

My primary passion is metallurgy.

Or it was, before Jonah.

For me, materials have always made sense. Metal and tongs. Not relationships.

The things I love would rust in the water.

All but Jonah.

The things I work with would be corroded by salt.

All but Jonah.

I roll out of bed. I light a candle. (What does Jonah do for light, I wonder, when he is inside of her?)

I pace the room. There is more water on my face, more salt.

(So deep?)

Back and forth, across the room, my candle lights everything.

(Surely, Jonah, there are no candles in the ocean?)

But I have something that he doesn't know.

So deep!

At my work table in the corner, under candle light, I review the project—recently completed—that has occupied so many of my working hours.

In the spring, a new invention arrived from Egypt: two bronze blades connected by a curved bronze strip. Ever since I observed it (so cunning! so delicate!), I had been determined to make a copy of my own.

Now, as I lift it—my own—the candle light flashes along the bronze.

I was always aware that there was someone else; I never believed myself to be a person to whom anyone would commit themselves entirely.

But *why*, Jonah?

Why a whale?

I pace again to the bed. Here, I see his eyes still—*still*—moving beneath his lids (would he dream for days?): water and salt.

I kneel by the bed. I set my candle on the floor. I again tangle one of my hands in his exquisite hair, through which the raw power flows: the gift of strength, breath, water.

With my other, I position the copy I have made: Egyptian genius, meticulously mirrored.

Passion meets passion. Two hands . . .

I am determined to proceed quietly; I would certainly never trouble his dream.

Only his reality.

I think: I am a land creature, Jonah, and I am a metallurgist (not that you ever cared) and I have a secret, too.

Scissors.

It Really Is All About You

Their telescopes detect it, when at last the world's technology permits them to—the light from the very center of the Universe.

"I told you!" you crow to the television when the announcement is made. "I always said!"

There it is, in fact, the picture on screen, written in pixels. Together, they comprise a set of unmistakable features, which in reality are many light-years in size: a body, a face, and a self, which is set against the backdrop of space.

It's You.

*

It is the most significant discovery that has ever been made. Bar nothing. As such, it triggers an intellectual and philosophical revolution. In every country, every city, it unleashes a sustained and anguished and energetic reevaluation of everything that was previously held to be true.

At least it does for everyone else.

But the discovery's greatest value to science and to people everywhere, and—still more importantly—to you, is the way that it serves as a clue (A Gigantic Clue!) that spurs the resolution of outstanding mysteries in many other fields.

Dark energy?

Dark energy, it is now clear, is the kineticization of the fact that your mother was a less-than-adequate mother.

Your mother's inadequacies are what cause the expansion of the universe to accelerate over time, rather than to slow down.

Dark matter?

Dark matter, which is far more abundant than normal matter, is the physicalization of the fact that your father was a less-than-adequate father.

Mysteries no more! The myriad and particular ways in which each of your parents mismanaged your upbringing are what the universe is controlled by and composed of.

This is what you were always telling everyone.

Once these things were invisible, unfathomable.

But everyone sees them now.

*

After this discovery, even phenomena that were once thought to be settled are shown to have been incompletely understood. Now, whenever the atom is split, the following particles—all previously undetected—invariably emerge:

• Your 8th grade math teacher, who made you feel slightly weird about math

• Your 9th grade history teacher, who repeated your embarrassing mispronunciation of "Tyco Brahe" in front of the entire class, slowly and skeptically and with cruel delight

• Your 10th grade civics teacher, who made you feel weird about yourself. Not in a sexual way, even—though that's what everyone would start to think, whenever you tried to tell them. So eventually you stopped trying to telling them.

Just weird about yourself, in a way that really stuck.

What does that even mean?

Let the scientists unpack that now!

Let them, as they discuss, write papers about it. And in every atom of these papers—in every page, in ever letter, in every molecule of pigment—let Mrs. Bryce and Mr. Decker and Miss Phillips be fundamentally embedded.

There.

*

What is light?

The answer is, of course, You.

But also: Simone.

You met Simone in college.

Simone encouraged you to keep your life expectations low. She told you authoritatively—you silly!—that journalism was not for you.

And what *would* have happened if she hadn't talked the pen out of your hands? What *would* have happened if she hadn't encouraged you not to write that first story, which, in her opinion, was "trivial and mean"?

Simone, who, nevertheless, for 40 years after that, after hurting you so, was your best friend.

How could such a thing even be possible? How could the person who infantilized, silenced, and betrayed you, the person who you never found it possible to forgive, the person for whom you always burned with a terrible woundedness and anger . . . *how could she also be your best friend?*

On some level, it is incomprehensible.

Yet it is also entirely true.

Importantly—or, rather: critically—your ambivalent connection with Simone lies at the heart of an otherwise enigmatic phenomenon: How can light be both a wave and a particle?

That is why.

Whenever you drew your curtains to block the light, whenever you had your solar panels repaired or installed new ones, and whenever you put on your sunglasses (back when you used to leave your apartment) you always thought of Simone.

That deep, underlying relationship, that profound causal coupling between your fraught friendship with Simone and the dual nature of light has always made sense to you.

Now it makes sense to everyone.

*

Black holes?

Those too.

At your sparsely-attended retirement party, your young coworker, Max, said something.

A quip.

In the moment he delivered it, you pieced it all together. You realized that Max had actually been making that same joke a lot. Over the past several years, as your hearing deteriorated and as the technological fixes required to compensate for that loss had become ever larger and more conspicuous, he had delivered it with increasingly cavalier confidence, certain that you would never hear him.

You'd thought he'd just been a mumbler.

But at the party, you had. When you'd paused in the middle of a story you'd been telling to have a bite of cake, you'd heard him deliver it in an exaggerated stage whisper. You'd heard it very clearly:

"Just because it happened to you doesn't mean that it is interesting."

In that moment, you knew that everyone in your office had long been laughing at you.

Black holes are the result of that indignity.

Inscribed into every black hole—fundamentally defining it—is what Max said. On each, lying on one side of every event horizon, it is drawn out in a curling cursive. It is written in gigantic letters, as large—literally as large—as it felt to you at the time:

J-U-S-T . . .

And so on, sublimely—significantly—through:

. . . I-N-T-E-R-E-S-T-I-N-G.

How uninteresting, eh, Max? you think.

Or possibly just ironic.

The kind of irony that bends space and time.

The kind of irony that not even light can escape.

Now, the scientists say "very, very interesting."

Everyone says that now. They say, "very, very interesting."

Everyone.

*

You follow with interest discoveries in many other fields as well.

Even when the revelations are unpleasant.

Geology, for example, is increasingly informed by many of the physical humiliations of your childhood.

The earth's magnetic pole? Because you were a bed wetter.

Volcanoes? All the times you picked your nose until it bled.

Plate tectonics? You'd prefer it, true, if no one knew . . .

Still: it is all You.

And who else can say that?

*

You, the center-of-the-universe You, leads them, at last, to . . . you.

Really, it was inevitable.

The molecules that compose the DNA of You are the size of planets. Using standard sequencing technology, it was initially difficult for scientists to get a read on a requisite number of As, Cs, Gs, and Ts. It was also difficult for them to scan Your ID card, which was hidden in Your gigantic wallet, beneath multiple layers of galactic cloth.

All science takes time.

So did tracking down the historical record of your parents (dead, but still living on, in their own way, via their effect on you, as the ultimate source of two of the most vital components of the universe). So did identifying what was shared by your dead teachers (better known by their subatomic identities), by Simone (also dead), and by Max.

But now they are coming to you.

They are converging on your doorstep, a mixture of reporters, scientists, and religious leaders.

You wait for the knock before you make your slow, slow, sweet way to the door.

You open it, just so slow.

"Why did it take you so long?" you ask.

*

It is so awkward.

So beautifully, beautifully awkward.

They laugh nervously. They smile.

"How are you feeling?" they ask you in many ways, in many voices.

"My oxygen tank is a little low," you say, gesturing to the container you trail behind you. You speak around the tubes in your nose.

Three of them are immediately dispatched on the errand of securing you more.

"My walker—" you begin, and a team of engineers, just so quickly, is summoned to optimize and repair it.

"How else may we help you?" they ask.

As the weeks pass, they bring you flowers. You like that.

You also like the daily calls from the world's presidents and prime ministers. You like the bright, emotional verses that are sung by the world's schoolchildren and piped in from classrooms on six continents.

You like it when they publish that story that you began to write so long ago. "Totally not trivial, totally not mean," they call it.

Even if they are lying.

Simone!, you think.

The lights flicker.

You like it when Max visits, day after day, fawningly apologizing.

Interesting, that.

You like, increasingly, the attention of the world's best doctors, who work to prolong you . . . even as you recognize that all of this attention is selfish.

What will happen to them, to everything, when you cease to be?

No one knows for sure. But they all observe it (and you watch them observing it): the shudder of everything. How close it all is to collapse. The way that, during your increasingly labored breaths, the outlines around everything are beginning to dim.

None of this can outlast you.

"Stay with us," they beg you, day after day. "Please don't die."

You wonder: Do you have a choice, even as no one else does? You, uniquely, among everyone? You, around whom everything else revolves? Could you find a way?

Probably.

You look at all of the people that are gathered around your bed and at the many others that are patched into your room by video. You look into their faces, which are both increasingly anxious and increasingly fuzzy.

You listen to the growing panic at the edge of their obsequiousness.

And you almost feel . . . something.

You wheeze heavily; you spit phlegm into the gemstone-encrusted bowl that has been personally crafted for your use.

Are you starting to feel something?
You give them a wry, spiteful smile.
Stars flicker; galaxies sputter.
"Everyone dies," you say philosophically, falling back onto your pillow.
Then you close your eyes.

Experimental Breeds:
Bears, Clothed in Rumpled Hoods, Pipe "Rapunzel" to the Sleeping Pigs

Generation 1

Rumpelstiltskin
x
Rapunzel

She was a woodland dwarf. Her eyes were dark and ancient, and her face was complexly wrinkled. As a prisoner of the king, she was confined to a tower, where she cut and spun her own hair.

This hair was lovely, part gold, part silk. It grew quickly, several meters per day. When harvested, it created shimmering fabrics, coveted by the well-to-do, and fetching fantastic prices.

As the dwarf cut and spun, her work was evaluated by a team of overseers, who tortured and abused her. They also hacked out her tongue.

"What is your name?" they would sometimes taunt her. They would laugh as she attempted to answer, degrading her with new brutality as her tongue stump twitched ineffectively.

"Duh-Duh," she responded.

The Emperor's New Clothes
x
The Pied Piper

In the center of the city lived a community of naked men. They preached a social anarchy, which was displeasing to the king. On Sundays, they dominated the city square, urging the abolition of the class system. Their chest hairs gleamed with their excited sweat and their buttocks twitched expressively.

One afternoon, the king's men, blaring military trumpets, raided the anarchists' compound. With royal whips, they lashed the naked men. The naked men bled. The marks of their injury, raw and dark, formed a sort of undergarment, which partly cloaked them.

After the lashing, the king's men bound the naked men's arms, then marched them through the city gates.

Outside the walls, the king's men executed the anarchists, then heaped them into a communal pit. As evening came, their bodies attracted vermin. Rats scurried across them, forming a temporary patchwork of outer garments: gray and white, black and brown.

Little Red Riding Hood
x
Sleeping Beauty

The wolf pricked the princess twice: first at her finger, then at her throat. Within moments, she fell into a deep sleep.

As she slept, she dreamed in fragments.

. . . of the prince who would one day wake her. He would be a tall, fair youth. He would wear a red cloak and have a masculine smile . . .

The wolf swallowed her.

. . . Her prince would ride a dark horse! He would hold a long, fierce sword. He would be determined to rescue her! And soon . . .

The wolf digested her. His stomach acid dissolved her; his intestines absorbed her.

. . . With romantic fervor, her prince would descend upon the evil creature . . .

What was in her was incorporated into new structures.

. . . Her prince would hack the monster open! . . .

She became wolf ears.

. . . Hacking and hacking—then methodically sifting—the prince would take her out . . .

And wolf eyes.

. . . Meticulously, he would remove all of her pieces. Even the tiniest! . . .

She became wolf fur and wolf teeth.

. . . And free her! . . .

She was exhaled as breath.

. . . Soon, he would come to her. At any moment . . .

She decayed into the soil.

. . . He would gallop . . .

From a riverbank, she was carried away by the current.

. . . His rage! His love! His blade! . . .

From the soil, she decayed into air.

. . . closer and closer . . .

She floated through the sky. For years, as she drifted, she continued to dream. And the longer she slept, the more fantastical her dreams become.

. . . When her prince came, no longer would he destroy only the wolf (not merely that!). Rather, he would defeat a still more formidable adversary: the true foe; the one that had cursed her even more cruelly . . .

What had once been her was now in all places, minutely distributed. What had once been her was now in all that was.

. . . The Second Law of Thermodynamics. He would overcome it! . . .

What had once been her was now in everyone.

. . . In conquering it, her prince would reconstruct her hands, her face, her dress, her everything. With a trillion kisses, he would repair her, infinitesimal part by infinitesimal part, until she became, once again, a beautiful princess, cloaked in her old garments, royal red . . .

And then she would open her eyes.

Goldilocks and the 3 Bears
x
The 3 Little Pigs

It began with an orgy, held in a field beyond the last silo, where barnyard bordered forest. There were two types of participants.

The first were domestic pigs, stout and splotchy-skinned. The second were bears, wild and burly, with thickly snarled pelts.

They were tender with one another. They kissed and petted. They tickled the protrusion between the lips and throat, naming it, with inane affection, the "chinny-chin-chin." They entwined their limbs, paws clasping hooves. They exhaled urgent suggestions, in disyllabic moans: "Harder, Hotter." At last, with convulsive shudders, they whispered, "Just Right."

In the morning, they dispersed. In the females' stomachs, the love continued to quiver, forming the incipient granules of new animals, part pig and part bear. In the pig mothers, these embryos were nourished by slop, consisting of porridge and bits of straw. In the bear mothers, they were nourished by a forest diet, consisting of leaf-topped sticks, golden-haired marmots, and ground squirrels.

From these materials, the pig-bear embryos constructed themselves, as might a builder. Methodically, they fashioned hearts and skin. With equal care, they laid the beginnings of lungs: intricate bellows, from which, at the moment of birth, they would violently exhale.

Generation 2

Rumpelstiltskin-Rapunzel
x
The Emperor's New Clothes-The Pied Piper

Years of atrocities fueled a hatred of the king. Amid the growing anger, two rebel factions emerged.

The first were the long-haired dwarfs. For generations, the king's guardsmen had threatened their hair, their freedom, and their honor. "Retribution!" the dwarfs now cried. "Revolution!" Mobilizing recruits and stockpiling weapons and supplies, they amassed a vast woodland army.

The second were the anarchists. They wore nothing—absolutely nothing—both to emphasize their iconoclasm and to protest the exploitative conditions in the king's textile mills. Calling themselves the "naked revolutionaries," they organized rallies and wrote speeches.

After the civil war, the two factions negotiated the outlines of a new republic.

What would they name it?

How would they rule it?

What kind of justice would they dispense?

As its first act—and how the common people cheered!—this new government executed the king and his men. Afterwards, it convened additional justice tribunals, tasked with determining the fates of lesser political criminals.

In the end, many of the remaining royalists were condemned to rot in an old bell tower. In this prison, they spun cloth for the republic: all one color. Rats gnawed at them. The tolling of the bells constituted a different kind of torture.

Spin, spin, spin.

Gnaw, gnaw, gnaw.

Clang, clang, clang.

Accustomed to lives of luxury, the convicted royalists were not stoic about their suffering. But their persistent moans and entitled pleas were, their gaolers agreed, very, very tiresome. And very, very loud.

So they cut out the prisoners' tongues.

Little Red Riding Hood-Sleeping Beauty
x
Goldilocks and the 3 Bears-The 3 Little Pigs

After several centuries, the story of Sheryl, the Eaten Princess, became a unifying national tragedy. Folk songs featured it; their titles included "Tomorrow, Tomorrow" and "The Prince that Never Came." Actors performed it, delivering moving soliloquies about her "hopeless vigil" and "irrevocable disintegration." Countrymen, upon taking leave of one another, often alluded to it. They used a traditional phrase, which was tinged with an ironical optimism: "May she yet emerge from the wolf."

A five hundred acre expanse, "Eaten Princess Park," also memorialized her.

During the summer, pilgrims converged upon on the Park. They burned incense and recited prayers. As gifts, they brought elaborate bouquets.

During the winter, the park was visited less often. From the pilgrims' gifts, loose bits of vegetation (nubs of sticks, wisps of straw) fell the earth and began to decay.

In the center of the park lay a vast—though empty—mausoleum, hewn from red sandstone. Fronting the entrance was her statue, made from the same stone. It depicted her at rest, whole and lovely, as she would have been, had she never been eaten.

Above the statue was the seal of her royal house, which depicted a pig and bear romantically embracing. About the park ranged the living emblems of this love. They consisted of two varieties: "pears," with pig snouts and clawed bear limbs, and "bigs," with bear muzzles and cloven pig hooves. Docile and sweet-tempered, they served as the "Spiritual Emissaries" of "Her Eaten Highness."

During the day, the animals foraged through the mausoleum, accepting treats of porridge from the visitors and Park wardens. At night, they curled at the base of Sheryl's statue, nuzzling lovingly at the stone. With small sobs, *Grroink, Grroink*, they seemed to mourn her. Their lungs worked, inhaling occasional pieces—bits of carbon, scraps of hydrogen—that had once composed her.

Generation 3

Rumpelstiltskin-Rapunzel-The Emperor's New Clothes-The Pied Piper
x
Little Red Riding Hood-Sleeping Beauty -Goldilocks and the 3 Bears-The 3 Little Pigs

It is a complex national emblem, composed of four faces, grouped into a single silhouette. Two, depicting the Eaten Princess and a sleeping pig-bear, represent the old monarchy. Two, depicting a long-haired dwarf and a naked bohemian, represent the revolution and the new republic.

The emblem summarizes a conflicted national feeling: admiration, first, for the divinely-appointed kings, and, admiration, second, for the upswell of common feeling, organized by the kings' victims, which had utterly obliterated these kings.

In the earth, there is another sort of memory, pressed into layers of clay. Near the surface are the marks of the Great Unrest. There are swords, red with both rust and ancient blood. There are fragments of propaganda, inscribed with dueling slogans; while the monarchists had cried, "Today, Today!" the rebels had shouted, "Tomorrow, Tomorrow!"

In a lower layer are the ruins of the old regime. Stones frame old ballrooms: vaulted chambers, through which silk-coated princesses had once promenaded, led by dainty pig bears. Amid these stones are the shreds of ancient tapestries, gold and white, and the remains of the once magnificent castle bells.

Mixed in the same strata, though less well-preserved, are the walls of peasant huts: thatches of straw, framed by wooden posts. Within these outlines are charcoal scraps, evidencing inadequate meals: bits of porridge, mixed with wolf gristle and rat skeletons.

In every layer, more confusedly, are a great jumble of human bones. They are large and small, elderly and infant, healthy and deformed. Each indicates its own tragedy. Some, the results of violence or deprivation, are profoundly horrifying; others, the results of age or illness, are merely routinely so.

Beneath these corpses, deeper yet, there are striations of sterile earth, which, preceding man, contain no stories.

The Anatomy of a Dream, Part 1
(Or: 10 Reasons Why)

1. You do not have a favorite animal. You never had one.
(You found—find—them all, truth be told, equally depressing.)
So why did people keep asking you that?

2. You never had a favorite fungus, a favorite plant, a favorite bacterium.

3. But you could *make* one.
A favorite.
And it would be your favorite, because you made it.

4. (As with desserts, or birthday presents, isn't homemade ever more heartfelt?)
((Even as—anyway—you never really liked the presents that other people gave to you. Or the desserts that they prepared. Even as your heart never really felt them.))

5. (((Not in comparison to what you could make, could dream of making.)))

6. ((((Theoretically.))))

7. But *this* would be your favorite because you made it.

8. *This.*

9. Because you made it.

10. (What else are hearts for?)

His Name-O

There was a farmer had a god, and Bingo was his name-o.

To appease Bingo, the farmer performed many sacrifices. Sometimes he sacrificed oxen, sometimes pigs. Dogs, though, were dearest to Bingo. Every growing season, the farmer purchased representatives of one of the sanctioned dog varieties, which had been bred by priests in the temple market. At planting, the farmer interred the animals' hearts, setting them between the rows of his seeds. Lifting his hands, he delivered a traditional prayer:

> *Bingo, make my fields fruitful.*
> *Bingo, bring rain.*
> *Bingo, accept this blood as your due.*

Every feast day, the farmer buried fresh hearts. If a wasting disease threatened his wheat, he watered them with new blood.

Most springs, in reward for his pious husbandry, the farmer enjoyed an excellent harvest. In the grain, speckles of the dogs' blood persisted.

In the summer, the farmer made bread and beer. Red tinged the bread's crust; in the beer's foam remained a taste of iron.

*

There was a farmer had a god, and Ingo was his name-o.

Over many centuries, as the "B" was dropped, the god became hungrier. He craved orthodoxy, in addition to blood.

During the holy wars, the farmer was conscripted into Ingo's army. An elite squadron of fighting dogs accompanied his division.

In battle, the dogs bit and tore, frenzied for Ingo. Many were martyred.

In the course of these same battles, the farmer lost one arm and one leg. Though these were serious sacrifices, they were not as honorable as martyrdom. They also made the farmer less useful.

The priests sent him home.

His wife was startled by his early return. Wouldn't he, she urged nervously, like to look over the fields with their sons? While she took a little time to prepare the house?

No.

Moving quickly despite his hobble, the farmer searched every room. By the fire, he discovered something truly shocking.

A cat.

His wife snatched up the forbidden animal, cuddling it close. Yes, she admitted, it had become a pet. But it was, all the same, a *sensible* pet. An affectionate pet. One that . . .

With his one remaining hand, the farmer ripped the cat from his wife's breast. With his one remaining arm, he dashed the animal's brains against the wall.

For days, his wife wailed like an unbeliever.

Every night, for three nights, the farmer went into his fields to pray. On his one remaining knee, he appealed to Ingo's Chosen—the spirits of the dogs who had been martyred.

On the third night, Ingo Himself answered. In the sky, His voice was a roll of thunder.

Dogs I have loved, but cats I have hated.

On the fourth morning, the farmer brought his wife to Ingo's priests. That afternoon, the community stoned her.

It was long and bloody. But the farmer also placed stones in his sons' small hands, so that they might also serve as instruments of Ingo's wrath and Ingo would not burn them.

*

There was a farmer had a god, and Ngo was his name-o.

Under Ngo's auspices, great ships were built. Distant lands were opened to the trade goods of Ngo's faithful and to the gospel of Ngo's missionaries.

Every year, the farmer exchanged a portion of his grain for equipment imported from distant lands: pipes for conveying water, blades for penetrating rocky soils, and potent new fertilizers.

Most important, though, were the slaves. After each new (and ever more productive) harvest, the farmer purchased additional slaves at the seaside market.

With their labor, the farmer was able to extend his farm into a plantation. To express gratitude for this bounty, the farmer selected passages from Ngo's hymnal.

He did not, however, care to sing them himself. The farmer's slaves had been forcibly removed from distant continents. The language barrier was therefore severe. In the beginning, the farmer found it difficult to persuade his slaves to pronounce the hymns' words correctly.

Eventually, however, these hymns became a daily ritual. Every afternoon, while one or more farm dogs slept at his feet, the farmer would sit on his balcony, frowning over one of his ledgers. Below him, his slaves labored, singing while they farmed:

Ngo, You are bountiful.
Ngo, You are merciful.
Ngo, we are grateful to learn Your Truth.

*

There was a farmer had a god, and Go was his name-o.

When the "N" was lost, the god became love.

To honor Go, the farmer gave his surplus grain to the hungry. He rescued maimed dogs and malnourished cats—animals that others had left to die.

His farm was a ragtag operation, never profitable.

Everywhere, however, the farmer saw the light of Go. He found it, gentle and personal, in the yellow wheat, the wet earth, and the spinning wheels of his tractor.

In church, the farmer experienced it in the form of ecstatic seizures. On the floor, among the pews, he would speak in a language he could not afterwards remember, in words that were not words, really—or even sounds—but rather the essence of Go (love that was light; light that was love):

Hinhin ududu hrug
Glalala fransfrans
Deedee reeree waw

In the wake of these euphoric fits, before human words returned to him, the farmer sometimes felt the comforting pressure of spirit fingers, invisibly entwined between his own.

It was the Hand of a Dear Friend.

*

There was a farmer had a god, and O was his name-o.

The farmer rarely thought of O. Not consciously. Language, though, had fossilized around the god. Without intending to, the farmer regularly invoked him.

"O!" he cursed when the Gen Mod Lab bungled one of his seed orders. "O!" he exclaimed, when his prize milker, a cow-goat chimera, kicked him squarely in the stomach. "O, O, O!" he cried at the moment of release, when embedded in the carapace of his robot wife. In a plot beside the farm, the farmer maintained a series of tombstones. Each commemorated a family farm dog: Claws, Clara, Bones, and all the rest. Beneath each name, eight traditional words were inscribed. It was a flourish that one would append to any death, and the farmer ascribed no literal significance to it:

May she rest in the arms of O.

*

There was a farmer had a god. But the god no longer had a name.

The farmer performed most of his work in a tissue culture hood. In laboratory dishes, he grew grain—pure grain, engineered for efficient *in vitro* growth. From it, the roots and stalks had been genetically excised.

In other dishes, the farmer grew dog meat—a commodity that, prior to the advent of victimless meat, there had existed no market.

But the farmer's meat had no face and no brain. It could not experience pain.

And it was delicious.

At his bench, the farmer engineered steaks using the muscle cells of border collies. He built hamburger patties with the adipose cells of bulldogs. He made sausages from the stem cells of Rottweilers.

Sometimes, in the rhythm of his work, the farmer would experience an inexplicable shiver. A sense of . . .

Presence.

During these moments, the farmer's stomach would flutter and his heart would go faster. Almost immediately, however, synthetic sensors in his bloodstream would fire, triggering the release of an additional nanoliter of FeelWell, an anti-anxiety agent.

Then the feeling would pass.

*

There was a farmer.

For three millennia, the farmer dreamed in stasis. As he slept, his ship crossed the outermost boundaries of the Intergalactic Republic. Behind it, it left a smear of light.

When the farmer woke, there was only emptiness. So he built a sun. Then a world to orbit it. Then water and air.

Afterwards, the farmer began to conjure the images that had accompanied him as he slept—creatures out of myth and history, which had long been absent from his restrictive home world.

Dreams.

He shaped the first into the planet's soft clay. Then he enlivened it.

When the creature woke, its eyes sparkled. With its tongue, warm and rough, it licked the farmer's hand.

"Dog," said the farmer, giving it a name.

Do I?

I am the only barber.

Outside, my iconic pole stands. It spins, but slowly enough that, if you are attentive—as all my customers must be—you can read the law painted onto it, red text onto white:

> *I shave all those, and those only, who do not shave themselves.*

In the morning, I shave two veterans: Greg, who lost both hands in the war, and Anders, who took a bullet to the spine.

Neither can shave himself.

I also shave Adam, whose patronship stems from a religious prohibition (laws within laws). Then I shave Paul, who feels that his hereditary wealth entitles him to the assistance of a domestic. But for this particular task (I am the only barber), he cannot hire a private manservant.

Read the pole.

At a mid-morning appointment, I shave a pair of identical twins, Raphael and Gabriel. Both are incurable pranksters. Today, they make a confession: Last night, over an unhealthy quantity of brandy, they conceived of a mad scheme to shave one another.

It hadn't worked.

As they relate this story, they laugh hysterically. But my smile is strained. "All those," I say sternly, then point to the pole through the window.

The law.

Self-shavers frequently skulk outside my shop. On their cheeks and chins—emphatically no work of mine—are irritated patches, bumpy and red. There are also many small cuts.

In the afternoon, one of these self-shavers scurries past my pole and into my shop, intent upon mischief of a different kind.

As if I would offer him a chair.

"Those only," I say, pointing again through the window. This time, however, the razor in my hand, naked and sharp, imbues my gesture with a second implication.

Get out.

Orville, who is afraid of razors, visits my shop at irregular intervals, never making an appointment. He comes again this afternoon. Shaking all over, he says that he "can no longer stand the sight" of himself. As I work, he closes his eyes and holds his breath.

But most of my customers elect to pay for my services because I am very good at what I do.

(They can see, anyway—as well as I—what those haggard, injured *self-shavers* look like, the ones who skulk outside.)

Many of them—admittedly—also come for the conversation.

In my shop, gossip flows. Even as I, personally, am famously discreet, my customers often share tidbits with one another: news about divorces, infidelities, and hunting trips. They talk about work: who's been laid off, who's been awarded a bonus, who's applying to what, and so on.

They also argue about politics and sports.

I—even I—have been known to speculate about tomorrow's big game.

After each shave, I ring the customer up at the register. (Even though the law does not specifically forbid it, I have never been able to bring myself to hire an assistant, either for clerical or janitorial tasks.) Then I wipe my scissors and razors clean and sweep the hair from the floor.

Not every man can be shaved in the morning. (I am the only barber.) Not every man—contrary to received wisdom—even wishes to be. So, today, like every day, I continue working until the evening settles. In the dimness, the white stripes of my spinning pole become more prominent than the red.

But the law is still visible.

The last customer lingers. In a way, he is new. But only in a way. I was his grandfather's barber. For nearly so long, I have been his father's and his uncles'. Now I am his.

When he was younger, he often accompanied his elders. He was an earnest boy. While his relatives gossiped, he waited patiently in one of the chairs at the front of the ship, absorbed in a book.

Now, he is an earnest young man.

Once he has paid, he continues standing at the counter.

"Mr. Barber," he says at last (he will not, as the rest of his family does, yet call me Frank).

"Yes?"

"I have been thinking about the law."

"The law," I say, and laugh a little. Out of habit, I glance through the window. At the same time, I reach up a hand to brush my chin.

It is smooth.

"I understand," he says, "all about 'all those'"—and here he gestures to one side—"and about 'those only'"—and here he gestures to the other. "But what about you?"

"I am well, thank you, Russell," I say, choosing, for both our sakes, to seem to misunderstand.

"But who shaves . . . ?"

"I will see you on Thursday," I say, shutting the register a little harder than I intend to.

"But—"

On the counter a razor sits. I lift it now. I initiate this action with the apparent intention of sharpening it, as I often do it the evenings. Or of returning it, clean and dry, to its proper drawer. But instead I weave it fiercely through the space between us—an act of apparent madness.

As if I am fencing with an invisible enemy.

Or shaving the air.

I flick my wrist one final time. Then I lower my arm.

When I look back at my young customer, he has taken a step back.

"I will see you on Thursday," I say.

His expression is bewildered. And fearful. And also a little hurt.

I meet it with a blank look.

"Yes, Mr. Barber," he says at last.

"Thursday," I repeat. Then, ostensibly out of habit—though, in reality, this time, I do it out of much more than habit—I point him to the pole.

But we both know that the solution to his question is not written there.

*

My apartment is connected to the back of my shop.

Inside my kitchen, I prepare supper. I sauté chicken in wine sauce. I steam white rice and boil broccoli.

After eating, I select one of the books from my shelf of classics.

My hands pass smoothly over the spines: Euclid, Euripides, Pascal. They date from a different time, before the world became

. . .

Complicated.

Tonight I choose Plato. The intellectual lines in this book are clean. Beautiful. Perhaps, as I read, I "immerse" myself in them. But I certainly do not lose myself.

With this book, I sit in a wooden chair beside the kitchen window. Outside, the pole spins.

I read until I am exactly the right kind of tired.

In my bed, I pull my sheets around myself, taut and smooth. I do not dream. My alarm wakes me just before sunrise.

In the bathroom, I stand before the mirror. My chin is ugly and imperfect; the night has has made it rough.

I do not like looking at it.

A barber, I know—the only barber—must always be presentable.

The light from the pole outside also penetrates the bathroom window; its light penetrates everywhere.

With a jerk, I pull the bathroom curtains tighter; I set the rug against the still fainter rays that extend beneath the door.

I cannot, of course, extinguish the law.

But I can dim it.

I remove my clothes. Perhaps, as I do, my heart is beating hard.

In the shower, I linger until the skin on my face is warm and soft and yielding. As I do, I square myself to what must come. Stepping out, I wrap myself in a towel. So that now . . .

When I stand again before the bathroom counter, my face is a blur.

I am not ready, for one can never truly be ready for this; and yet also I am . . .

Ready.

"I—" I scream, through the roar of it, the happening: the portal in the bathroom wall, which both does and does not open; my fingers, which both clench and not clench; the figure, which both does and does not emerge from that portal, as I both do and do not lift my hand.

Snow White
and the Seven Biblical Floods

1.

Snow White fled into the forest.

"I have sinned!" she cried, knocking at the first cottage she came to. "In His eyes, I am one of the wicked!"

The first of the brothers, Pride, answered the door with a grand flourish. "God will never find you here!" he promised.

"Yes, yes!" concurred Lust in a rather different tone. "Stay with us!"

"But you must cook for us," said Gluttony.

"And work in the mine," said Greed.

"And withhold nothing from me . . . " said Envy.

" . . . Or ever, ever displease us," growled Wrath.

("What?" slurred Sloth from one of the interior rooms.) From the doorstep, Snow White gave the brothers a grateful—if tentative—smile. But then it began to rain.

2.

The King and Queen of Heaven were determined to cleanse the earth. But they could not agree on how to do it.

"Let's drown everyone," said the King said.

"Let's poison them," said the Queen.

"Your way would be too slow!" objected the King. "Your way would be too wet!" counter-objected the Queen.

More discussion followed. The King observed that the Queen's plan served as evidence that she was deeply stupid—too stupid, perhaps, to remain a member of the Celestial Court. The Queen disputed this observation. If anyone's right to membership in the Celestial Court were to be reassessed, shouldn't it be the

King's? Because didn't his own plan (a plan based on . . . what? on water??), which he continued not merely to defend but to cling to, even though a clean and sensible alternative—her plan—already existed, constitute far more compelling evidence of stupidity?

Hard eyes.

Heavy breathing.

Stalemate. Finally, the Queen proposed a reconciliatory picnic.

"Would you like an apple?" she asked the King.

3.

The weather was getting bad. To preserve the dwarfs, Snow White commissioned a boat.

Up the gangplank she led them, two by two, representatives of all seven dwarf-kinds.

"Come on now, Bashfuls," she urged them, after the sea journey had continued some weeks. "You can mate, too!"

With a smile, she pointed to what the Happys had just begun to do with one another, right there on the deck. And to what, lying spent, the Grumpys were just now completing.

The Bashfuls, a female and a male, looked uncertainly at Snow White.

They looked at the Happys. And the Grumpys. Then briefly, blushingly, they looked at one another.

Then they looked away.

4.

"Fairest!" cried the Queen, affronted and astonished by the image her Mirror returned to her.

How had a planet grown fairer than she?

"A flood!" she decided, and, as she lifted her fingers, her curse passed through them.

Rain, rain, rain.

Once the green portion of that distant—and in her own view, really quite ugly—planet had been submerged, and what remained was only blue, she gave the Mirror a smug look.

But still she waited.

By the fortieth day, innumerable bodies had risen to the surface of the water, bloated and disintegrating. Their smell was putrid; their color was gray.

She decided to pose her question again.

"It is you, O Queen," returned the Mirror.

5.

Her Prince, the Prince of Heaven, had said that she was the only woman for Him. All the rest were disgusting whores.

So Snow White endured the forty days and nights of genocidal rain. When everyone else was dead, He descended to her on a carpet of rainbow.

After the terror of her time in that little boat—after the weeks of frightful loneliness—her lips met His, hungry.

"Easy," He said—a laugh.

"Easy!" He repeated. But when she kissed Him yet again, He pushed her violently away.

"How?!" He growled.

"My Lord . . . ?"

"Tell me, Miss Snow White," He said—and now his tone was perfectly ghastly—"how is it that you have learned to kiss so well?"

Then He threw her into the sea.

6.

Two of every kind, He commanded them.

"Heigh-ho!" agreed the erstwhile miners.

At His decree, they exchanged their wheelbarrows and pick axes for cages and collecting nets. Then, obediently—if not exactly wholeheartedly—they devoted themselves to their new profession.

For ten days.

Twenty.

Thirty.

"I am His servant," said Doc in a low tone, looking surreptitiously at the sky. "And yet sometimes . . . "

"I miss the diamonds," agreed Dopey, darting an anxious look upward. Above his head, as a sort of shield, he held what remained of the arm that the lioness had eaten.

"I miss the emeralds," said Sleepy in a woozy whisper. On his hand, a pair of small bite wounds oozed a venomous green.

" . . . rubies . . . " rasped another dwarf, so severely mauled that the others found it difficult to remember what his name had originally been.

Now they called him "Bleedy."

7.

"He's dead," the hunting doves reported. They staggered beneath the weight of His immense Heart, which they had brought back as proof.

At Snow White's feet—Thump!—they let It fall.

"You have done well," said Snow White. One by one, as she beckoned, the doves hopped onto her fingers. One by one, she sponged them clean: their fierce beaks first and then their lovely feathers. So much blood.

Only when the birds were clean did Snow White brave a glance toward the center of the grove, where the Mirror was mounted.

The Mirror returned to her her own reflection.

Snow White—not God—was now "The Cruelest of Them All."

Her eyes filled with tears.

"I had to issue that order," she said. "I had to stop—"

Her voice broke.

As the doves nuzzled her consolingly, she let her gaze drift past the Mirror, past the grove and its trees, to everything beyond.

To the dwarfs' cottage, which lay at the bottom of the hill. To the palace in the distance, where she'd been born, and to the great city that surrounded it, with its tens of thousands of inhabitants. To all the world that existed beyond that, both the wild spaces and the civilized ones, which were filled with living creatures that He had been determined to drown.

As she wept, she wondered:

What would this new world be like?

What could a world BE like, without God?

"Look!" cooed one of the hunting doves, one wing pointing up.

Snow White looked . . . and gasped.

In the sky, a new structure had emerged, lovely and glittering: a diaphanous semicircle composed of diverse bands of light.

A rainbow.

From the grove, all of the doves fluttered up to meet it—clean feathers against a blue sky.

Snow White smiled.

Though it felt like a sign, she knew that it could not be. Now that God was dead, there could no longer be signs from Anyone.

This was simply something beautiful.

The Anatomy of a Dream, Part 2
(Or: 8 More Reasons)

1. Who doesn't hate incest? But *your* hatred is somewhat beyond what is usual.

For you, the idea of a hamster pairing with another hamster makes your stomach turn.

Two near-identical creatures, coupling; two creatures that look the same, together, like that, making more . . .

It doesn't matter how many generations separate them, or what sort of cousins they are: 15th, 27th, or 100th.

That isn't the point.

You experience this in your stomach. But it's not as if emptying it would relieve the feeling. You could, in fact, keep heaving and heaving, but it wouldn't ever *fix* it; it wouldn't ever ease . . .

If only, instead, that hamster could be persuaded to choose a mate that were very, very different from it.

Like a capybara. (At least a capybara!)

Or, even better: a kangaroo.

Or a lobster.

Or a slime mold.

Or a bacterium.

Or . . .

2. You grew up watching *Rocky and Bullwinkle*. (Didn't everyone?)

At the time, and for years and years afterwards, you dreamed of staging your own sequel, featuring the children, Rinkle and Bully, that the two protagonists never had, not literally.

Not on screen.

"Must merge moose and squirrel," you would say in a Boris accent—an accent that, over the years, as you have continued to practice it, has become better and better.

And if you were to succeed in this, as Boris never did, you would not be the villain.

If you were to do this.
When.

3. Here's a letter that you wrote to Aesop the other year, before learning that he was dead:

Dear Aesop,
If we surgically conjoin the tortoise and the hare, then
both of them can race as one.

4. You've always wanted to make a difference. And by "make a difference," you've always meant "make things really different."

5. Other people have other ideas about what your sports team's mascot needs to be. Those people are wrong.
You, in contrast, understand exactly what will be required.
Something intimidating . . .
. . . but also quirky.
Like a bear-chipmunk.
Or a lion-parakeet.
Or, or, or.
And won't the fans cheer all the louder, when you trot out a real specimen at halftime?
Won't they scream?

6. Must merge moose and squirrel. Must merge moose and squirrel. Must merge moose and squirrel. Must . . .

7. Biodiversity, to other people, is a solemn row of catalogs, everything to its assigned container.
But you see it as an opportunity for cultural exchange.
Or maybe as a potluck.
Or a party.
Or, anyway, it *could* be.
So why—and this part has never made any sense to you: never, never, never—*why*, so much of the time, do so many of the guests remain sitting on the sofa, shyly focused on their own appendages, making no eye (or perception-based) contact at all?

Why aren't they talking to one another?
Why aren't they . . . dating?

8. In your dreams, you are a mer-person. Your spine extends into a fish's tail. By pumping it, you move powerfully through the water.
You have never felt so complete, or so perfect.
But then you wake up.

The Evolutionary Alice

"Who are YOU?" the Caterpillar asked Alice. And well he might ask, for the two of them had last shared an ancestor eight hundred million years ago, and there was a great deal to catch up on.

So Alice explained herself. And she did it very prettily, as she might have done at school, hands folded in the recitation. To the tune of "Twinkle, twinkle little mammal," she recited the story of bones (five hundred million years ago) and hair (two hundred million years ago). And she was just about to begin a verse about lactation—which she thought was rather good—when the Caterpillar silenced her with a faceful of smoke, Puff! Puff! Puff!, shaped into many colored rings.

As Alice left off, coughing, the Caterpillar launched haughtily into a new subject: embryonic development. He maintained that, as an arthropod—and, more particularly, as a protostome—he was fundamentally superior, since the first opening to his digestive tract, as an embryo, had been his mouth.

"Proto," he explained coldly, meant "first." And "stome" meant "mouth."

Alice, faltering, was forced to confess that, like other creatures with bones, she was a deuterostome. That is: second-mouth. So, as an embryo, the first opening in her digestive tract had not been the mouth, but instead something more vulgar.

"Who ARE you?" asked the Caterpillar. This time, though, it was no longer a question, but instead a sneer.

But, just as Alice was becoming quite flustered—and possibly a little angry, too—she caught sight of a familiar streak of white. When she turned her head, there he was again. "White Rabbit! White Rabbit!" Alice called. For, after her unpleasant conversation with the Caterpillar, she felt an even warmer connection with the Rabbit. Not only were they both deuterostomes (and mammals, too), but their ancestors—curiouser and curiouser—had split ways only ninety million years ago, in the mid-Cretaceous, and so they were practically cousins.

"Wait!" Alice cried. Down the forest path, she pursued the Rabbit, intent upon his bobbing ears and elegant waistcoat. But, in her hurry, she caught her foot on something hard and strange, and she fell heavily.

As she retook her footing, one knee smarting, she locked eyes with the curious object—the animal, actually—with whom she had collided.

It was not a mammal. But it was, at least, a deuterostome, and a tetrapod, too—a four-legged creature—descended, like her, from a not-quite-fish, whose ancestors had emerged from the sea.

A Turtle.

"Pardon me," Alice said to the Turtle—or, as she now saw, more precisely, a Mock Turtle, who stood, in fact, at the edge of the path, at the bank of a lake of mock turtle soup. Its shell was still dripping with broth and boiled vegetables.

Amid curtsies (her knee hurting worse, each time she bent it), Alice explained that she had to be going.

The Turtle, for its part, did not seem in the least moved by any of this: no more emotionally invested in her departure than he had been in her arrival.

Well, Alice thought: That was reptiles for you.

Up the path she hurried, calling after the Rabbit. But she had lost all trace of him.

Soon—worse luck—she came to a fork in the way. It was a juncture that reminded her of a branch point in the Tree of Life, a place where two species diverged from a common ancestor.

. . . And she had no idea which path to take.

Suddenly, however, Alice had a mad idea. Perhaps, she thought, the most sensible thing, just now, would be to model her own behavior after that of a biological population, engaged in a blind act of evolution.

So Alice selected a direction at random. The left. Then, eyes closed, she proceeded stumblingly, trying, as she went, to think as little as possible about where she *might* be going. An evolving population certainly wouldn't.

After a few paces, sensing that the path had widened, Alice opened her eyes, and . . .

No White Rabbit.

Instead, she found herself in a grove, which contained a long table, set for tea. From the head of a table, a bright-eyed hare—a March Hare—bounded up from a chair. Then, in an eager voice, while his paws trembled a little, he asked: Was Alice, by any chance, a bilaterian?

It was a spectacularly foolish question. Alice couldn't help herself: she laughed very rudely. Because of course she was a bilaterian. Wouldn't that—she thought—have been perfectly evident to anyone? Didn't she have bilateral symmetry? Didn't her left side mirror her right? And, anyway, the vast majority of animals were bilaterians. In fact: only quite distantly related— and oddly patterned creatures: things like jellyfish—weren't.

But, as Alice laughed, the March Hare retained such an earnest and expectant expression that at last Alice began to regret her impertinence.

"Yes," she said finally.

Oh, my! The March Hare was delighted to hear that! Because today, he said—like every day—he and his friends would be celebrating the 800 millionth Birthday of the Urbilaterian, the last common ancestor of all of the bilaterians! Would Alice like to join the celebration?

Really, Alice would rather have not. But she hesitated, just a moment, and in that moment the March Hare took her arm, and soon they were both whirling about the table, faster and faster. "A Very Merry Urbilaterian Birthday to You!" he sang. "A Very Merry Urbilaterian Birthday to All of Us!"

As they whirled, Alice perceived that this was a very small party. In fact, there seemed to be only one other celebrant: a Dormouse, which was seated in a chair at the far end of the table. At first, the rodent seemed to be deeply asleep. But as the Hare, pulling Alice, sped past, he gave the Dormouse's chair a little whack. At that jolt, the rodent's eyelids fluttered, and he began to sing wheezily: "Twinkle, twinkle, little bat . . . "

Then, suddenly, as if summoned, a bat—a Bat!—emerged from the Dormouse's tea cup. Flapping its wings, it began its own circuit of the table.

"Flying mouse! Flying mouse!" cried the March Hare.

To Alice, this was all spectacularly upsetting. For, of course, in an evolutionary sense, "flying mouse" was a complete fallacy. In fact, bats were not even particularly closely related to mice; instead, they were *more* closely related to carnivores: creatures like cats.

"But—!" she interjected, as she bobbed behind the Hare. "But—!"

"Flying mouse!" the March Hare repeated, louder than before.

To Alice, there was little that was so irksome—next, of course, to taxonomic errors—as not being listened to. But then . . .

"A Cheshire Cat!" cried Alice. For there *was* a cat—just such a cat—on the far side of the grove. And this cat seemed to be floating—an airborne condition that was entirely at odds with what Alice knew of mammals, with, again, just the bats excepted.

"Mr. Cat!" said Alice. And, with a furious little shrug (which had not very much, it must be said, in common with a curtsy), she shook herself free from the March Hare's paw and went racing after.

As Alice ran up the path, the strains of "A Very Merry Urbilaterian Birthday to You!" became ever fainter. Then, suddenly, just as Alice was about to catch up to the Cat, the animal stopped abruptly. Turning to her, he asked, "Do you play croquet?"

Alice did, of course. And indeed—yes!—when Alice looked ahead, to where the Cat was pointing, she saw a wide field, set with a great quantity of wickets, as if for a tournament. But it was, assuredly, the maddest form of croquet that Alice had ever seen. Instead of mallets—flamingos. And, instead of balls—hedgehogs.

But, to Alice, the most unsettling part of this game was the players themselves. Which, though alive, seemed, all the same, to be . . .

Playing cards.

And while Alice, dumbfounded, tried to make sense of *that*— Where, if anywhere, did these creatures even belong on the Tree of Life? (And the prospect, frankly, that they might not even belong to the Tree of Life was by far the most distressing idea Alice had encountered all day)—one of the flamingos lurched toward her.

It was, like all birds, a cousin of the Mock Turtle. But, as the flamingo set itself between her hands, as if determined to serve as her mallet, Alice immediately decided that she liked this bird even *less* than she had liked the Mock Turtle.

At least the Mock Turtle had not been presumptuous.

By then, a hedgehog was nudging Alice's foot, as if equally determined to be her ball. Alice shot a pointed look in the Cat's direction, hoping that he might have a word with it. Cats, after all, together with bats, were the cousins of hedgehogs, and it was only to be expected—wasn't it?—that they might take a little responsibility for them. But the Cat had disappeared.

Still, why not play? Ordinarily, Alice was very good at games. But she soon discovered that, as eager as the animals had been to play *with* her, they did not wish to help her play *well*. The first took great delight in going limp whenever Alice raised it; the second, giggling, would always unroll exactly when she wished to strike it.

All in all, both were a good deal sillier and more spitefully uncooperative than Alice generally preferred her birds, mammals, or croquet equipment to be.

Finally, just when Alice was beginning to become *quite* frustrated, she felt a tap on her shoulder. Turning around, she found . . .

"Mr. Cat!"

Smiling broadly, the Cat pointed to a conspicuously regal card, who stood a short distance down the field, surrounded by courtiers.

The Queen of Hearts.

"I suspect you won't like her," said the Cat.

"Why not?"

But the Cat only smiled. So Alice—trying, but failing, to set aside her flamingo—edged closer. And listened. And found, to her distress, that the Queen was discoursing, very wrongheadedly and bombastically, on a topic that was dear to Alice's heart—the origin of species.

Every species, the Queen was explaining, had been created separately and by a Supreme Intelligence. All in one day.

"I told you wouldn't like her," said the Cat.

The Cat was perfectly correct; Alice did not.

Now, Alice pushed her flamingo away very forcefully. (Perhaps even a little rudely.) With a squawk of indignation, it lurched away from her.

Good riddance.

With her own—and far greater—indignation, Alice began to push her way through the Queen's entourage: a medley of 7s, 8s, and 9s, who were staring at the Queen with rapt expressions. But whether they were too frightened of the Queen to dispute her account, or were simply dreadfully stupid, Alice couldn't be sure.

"Your Majesty!" Alice cried, once at the front. Then, with a small curtsy, she launched into a new verse, called "Descent with Modification."

For just a moment, the Queen simply stared, as if too astonished to speak. But soon her color changed, becoming apoplectically purple. Then, extending a trembling finger, she bellowed, "Off with her head!"

"Run," the Cat suggested.

So Alice did.

Across the green she fled, through the balls and wickets and the other players, through the hedgehogs and flamingos. When she turned her head, she could see a phalanx of card soldiers a short distance behind, Jacks and 10s at the fore, each carrying a menacing scythe.

At the far end of the course, the way was blocked by a wall of rose bushes, which were very oddly colored: red paint, splashed over white petals.

But there was nowhere else to go. And no time to think. So Alice plunged into the bushes.

As she fought her way through, she was torn by thorns. And smeared by paint. And brought up short, suddenly, by a vision—

The ancestor, 1.5 billion years dead, that linked her with these roses. A faceless, one-celled creature, magnified, here, many millions of times. An ancestor, spherical and translucent, that had arisen before the invention of limbs. Or eyes. Or heads.

("Off with her head!" came the shouts from behind.)

"Plant-Animal Matriarch," Alice whispered. "I—"

At that moment, though, there was a terrible lurch, and the ground gave out beneath her. And Alice found herself falling—falling, falling, falling—together with a great quantity of roses.

"Cousins!" she screamed, as the flowers swarmed around her. "Oh, distant cousins!"

Then, with a start, Alice woke up. And she found, to her astonishment, that she was seated in a meadow, against a familiar tree—the very tree she had fallen asleep beside. Had it been only a short time before? And there was her sister, just a few feet away, still reading aloud from *On the Origin of Species*.

"Oh, sister!" Alice exclaimed, hopping up from the ground. "I feel as if I've been away for millions of years!"

Her sister laughed. Under normal circumstances, Alice would have found that very irritating. But, at that particular moment, in the joy of being safe—with her head, still, attached to her neck!—it all felt warm and reassuring and right, and Alice was glad of it.

"Let's go home," she entreated.

So away they went together, arm in arm, talking animatedly, into the warmth of the summer afternoon. And when, down the path, the trees thinned and they sighted the house at the bottom of the hill, Alice broke into a run, pulling her sister, still laughing, along behind. For there in the doorway stood their last common ancestor—still very much alive—a woman whom they both simply called "Mother."

Seventh Date

I had been hurt before—deeply, deeply hurt.

So, even when we had been together for several weeks and he had been nothing but attentive (even, by some measures—though not mine—excessive), I was still insecure.

And even when he had lain heaps of gifts on my doorstep and had surprised me with candles, burning with a perfume that he knew I liked, and when, evening after evening, he had passionately serenaded me, his songs so loud that the entire neighborhood could hear (honestly, though, I loved that too), I was still insecure.

And when, even in this ardor, there were still private notes, intimate and sensual and pitched just for me, so that, when I received them, I shivered, as if at a kiss, and when he had shown me, again and again, how intensely he cared, I was still insecure.

And when he had done so much, for the sole purpose of impressing me, of assuring me, and of proving . . .

Still.

*

That evening, I came to his doorstep. The sun was setting. That night—our seventh date— we planned to see the stars. (Perhaps, if things progressed that way, we would pass the hours until morning among those stars.)

But I arrived early.

*

"I am jealous," I had warned him from the beginning. I had said that on our first date, on our second date, on our third.

*

I knocked softly. It was our private knock.

No answer.

The knob was stiff; it did not turn. The outer door was secure,

which made me think . . .
I wondered.
But locks do not stop a curiosity like mine.

*

"And I am faithful," he had said.

*

Down the hallway I proceeded softly. But my softness was different now. My softness was more immediate and less tender.
There are many ways to be soft.
(Soft!)

*

"Promise me," I had implored him, after every gift, after every song, "that I will be your only."

*

Further down the hallway, I heard sounds. It was like a . . . song.
But it was not a song I recognized.
This was a new song.

*

And he had promised.

*

Perhaps, for my sake, he was practicing this song. Perhaps later, to please me, he would perform it.
Perhaps.
But I am not good at waiting.

*

"Do not hurt me," I had warned him.

*

Soft! Soft! Down the hallway, I followed the sounds, faster and faster.
Where the hallway ended, there was another door. An inner door. (Here, the song was loudest!) Beneath it, through the crack above the floor, something gleamed.

*

I had warned him. When I had, I had been talking half to him and half to the past: to the man in the garden, to the man by the sea.

*

The door's handle was stiff, as the first's had been. Locked.

*

"Do *not* . . ." I had begged him.

*

But locks do not stop me—I have said that already—or a love like mine.

A love?

(Could I call it love?)

I could call it whatever I liked!

*

And he had said that he wouldn't, not ever.

*

I forced the door open. Splinters crunched against hinges (soft! soft!). Then the room's interior flashed back at me: bright, bright, bright. But he was there too. He was singing, and he was on his knees.

But—O!—he was more than singing. He was more than kneeling. He was . . .

Cavorting! Copulating! With . . .

. . . another. With the source of all this brightness! But how his motions (treacherous! perfidious!) shifted when he saw me.

(If he had not been on his knees before!)

And his sounds . . . ?

Gibbering denials, blubbering apologies, hysterical pleas.

Did he think I had not heard it before?

Did he think that I would listen?

"No others!" I said, in echoes of the past, "No others! No others!"

And this . . . And this . . .

. . . *Other*. It was inert and crude. It was tawdry, cheap, and glittery. It was shaped like . . . not a woman, not exactly. And not like an animal, not exactly. But it certainly was bright.

But I never showed you the stars, did I, darling? I never showed you . . .

Because I am brighter, my dear one.

I am brighter!

"Forty years!" I screamed at him. "In the desert! In a whale! Fields scorched; a wasting famine, down to bones and skin! And floods, higher than you can breathe, deeper than you can swim; a fall from the highest tower in the world; locusts and boils and a withering curse, passed through your loins, out to seven generations! To seventy!"

He cowered against the tawdry gleam of his *Other*: his idol, his thing, his golden strumpet, his *it*. No words anymore. No pleas. He cowered there, as if . . .

"Misery!" I screamed. "Forever and ever and ever!"

But in fact these were all simply manners of speaking, articulations of a leniency that I had no intention of according him.

I lifted my hands through a pain that was beyond speaking; I held them high as lightning gathered at my fingers.

Smite!

Smite!

Smite!

. . . until he was ashes: dead beyond dead, dust beyond dust. And his *Other* was smashed and molten (and who would worship it now?) and all its gleam had boiled away.

Everything lost. Everything broken. All dust and rubble.

I dropped my hands. Then I fled that cursed place, sweeping back through the smashed-in doors and the splintered locks.

Out into the setting sun I continued, and from there into darkness. Then I went deep into the pinwheels of nighttime fire, amid all the stars that I had intended to show to him.

I would, I vowed, never look back. I would stay here, far above, nursing this.

I would remain here, grieving.

How *can* one heal, when one has been so betrayed?

One never heals.

How *can* one trust again, when trust has been so broken?

One never can.

*

But.

*

I felt him, another him, before I turned; I felt him, before I looked.

I chose him, before I turned, out of all the others.

I saw him, before I turned, and I saw, too, all of the beautiful things that we might make together.

Maybe this time.

I *knew*, before I turned.

And then I turned.

*

I speed to him now, heart in my mouth, heart at my lips. I alight beside him.

Soft.

Amid the leaves that are close to him, my form is a curl of fire, like a golden flower. Then I am a chain of such flowers, spreading across the green. More and more, until he feels the heat of it, hears the crackle.

And he turns.

I have only one line by which to pick up patriarchs. I have never needed to craft another. And I say it now, fierce and tender, while his ear bends to me, for fear and awe, and his lips part and his heart beats, quick with wanting.

I say it now, smoldering and bright:

"I am your God."

The Anatomy of a Dream, Part 3
(Or: 6 More Reasons)

1. Griffins.

The best of animals, part lion and part eagle (the noblest of the animals, the bravest and most worthy) are restricted to the human imagination, trapped inside the heads of dreamers like you. This has been true for centuries.

But maybe you can let them out.

2. Who can't set a bone? Who can't remove a gallbladder?

That is not the sort of "doctor" that you want to be.

YOU, rather, will be a Ph.D.: the sort of doctor who dreams of and creates things that never existed before.

To your white-smocked assistants (whose fear you will have long since earned), you will issue instructions, breezy but firm.

You are going to need some sunflower chloroplasts, you will say.

Then you are going to need a water buffalo.

3. As nimble as a hummingbird, as indefatigable as a tortoise. What an exceptional soldier this proposed creature would be!

If you possessed such an army . . .

4. Other commitments are superficial: the sexual partners we chose (for those that choose them), the people we marry (for those that marry).

Air gaps divide us, ultimately.

If, though, your cells were to be intermingled with an iguana's, with a koala's, with a salamander's (with, with, with), and together you were to compose one body?

No gap.

Every part of this commitment would perforce become visceral. Every part would be deep.

No gap, no gap.

No gap-no gap-no gap.
Nogapnogapnogapongap.

5. Like a dog, it will be loyal and energetic. Like a cat, it will be sleek and elegant and capable of disposing of its own wastes.

It will sell, this breed, with the French-seeming name you will give to it: "D'ghat."

D'ghat!

D'ghat!

Once you have completed the first—once you have, by creating it, created a market—it will sell, sell, sell.

Howl-purr, bark-meow.

Who would not fundamentally adore this: half-dog, half-cat?

(And sell and sell and sell.)

Die, kill, swoon, accept bankruptcy, at the prospect of possessing it?

(And sell and sell and sell.)

6. Nature is a jock, thick-headed and beautiful. Everyone loves it.

Every afternoon, you pump iron, preparing. One day, when you are strong enough, you'll slam it up against its locker and punch it in the face, then shout something withering, like: "Overrated!"

Then—cool as anything—you'll walk away.

The Princess and the Pond

Contract magic was the most powerful kind of magic: magic integrated with legality.

Contracts were inviolable.

Now, since both had signed; now, since the Princess had paid what she had promised (and how she had paid!), no power in the world could reverse an article.

There was no going back.

"I have always hated your family," the Witch had said. But the Witch, per the contract, had been obligated to give the Princess exactly what she wanted.

However much it may have galled her.

Now, the Princess was human. Now, she had legs and a complete set of fashionable, place-appropriate clothes: a dress, a jacket, a scarf, a hat, and a pair of gloves.

Now, her gill slits had closed over, leaving no mark at all.

Now, as she was waiting for the prince—*her* prince—to come, she was dancing.

Dancing!

Over the surface of the pond, she glided. Through the glittery air, she twisted and spun. Each time, returning to the ice, her landing was graceful.

Whenever the Princess looked down, catching her reflection in the ice, she confirmed that she was beautiful. And not merely beautiful—for she had always been that—but beautiful according to the metrics of the people of this world.

Beautiful in the only way that mattered.

And hadn't she earned it?

Earned it, first, with all the research that she had done. For weeks, after saving the prince's life, she had studied his world. From a hole in the ice she had watched the pond's human visitors, assisted by a clever periscope made of pond reeds.

Afterwards, she had recorded her findings in terms of what she wanted. Using legal inks harvested from the bodies of aquatic worms, she had set down everything she required, point by point, over 60 rolls of an algae paper scroll.

Then—*Poof!*—the Witch's magic had made it real.

It was all in the contract.

Now, wind was flowing through the Princess' hair. Now, her dress was fluttering in the air, quickly and lightly. And *yes*, she thought, as she slashed across the ice, it was worth it; it was *still* worth it, even if . . .

There had, of course, been a second part to earning this, a second half to the contract, the half that the Witch had written out.

The far more difficult half.

"I have always hated your family," the Witch had said.

And indeed the Witch had (indeed, she had!) because she had insisted on being paid in the form of the magical scepter that belonged to the Princess' father. Through this scepter, she had, in effect, demanded the entire Pond Kingdom: all the water that lay beneath the ice.

The Princess had delivered it.

(Stolen it.)

Now, thought the Princess, as she raced across the pond, faster and faster, her father would be suffering. Assuredly, the Witch had already imprisoned him. (Tortured him?) Or worse . . .

Of course—let it not be forgotten (the Princess certainly would not be!)—it hadn't *needed* to be like this. Her father could have helped her. But he hadn't. Instead, he had laughed at her. "Above the water?!" he had sneered, as if nothing worth having existed there. "A *man*?!" he had scoffed.

He could have behaved differently. But he hadn't.

It had been a terrible price. The Princess felt the hurt of it now, just a little, in her new throat. Something sharp, when she breathed . . .

But now—anyway—there, in the distance, didn't she see . . .

A speck?

She cut her twirl short.

The Prince?

And while her new heart beat . . .

It was him!

. . . she slashed up a spray of frozen flakes, and came to a perfect stop at the center of the pond.

The Prince.

She had fallen in love him after he had fallen into her world through a crack in the ice. At first, as she had heaved him onto the surface, he had been unconscious. But then his eyelids had fluttered and their eyes had met. (Their eyes had met!) Then, even though she'd known that, to his people, her people were either monsters or they were food, she had been tempted to remain. (Briefly, madly, she had been tempted!)

Still—all the same—she had pushed herself back toward the opening in the ice.

But then, just as she had slipped back into her own world, he had called out to her.

(He had called out to her!)

Love.

After that, for weeks, dreaming of him, she'd returned to the surface again and again. Through her periscope, she'd seen that he, just like her, had come back every day.

From the first moment she'd seen him, that day of the accident, she'd known that he was a prince. Royalty recognizes royalty. But each time he'd returned to the pond, she'd learned more that had confirmed it.

That castle in the distance?

It belonged to his family.

Each time, he, like her, had seemed restless and troubled. It was as if he were pining for her, the way that, in the stories, human men sometimes do, when you are to their distorted memories a woman of their world. It was as if he were wasting away for the lack of her, as human men were said to do, when you have saved their lives but they have not correctly ascertained what you are.

Had he been pining?

And today? Now that she was human?

She'd *known* that he would come. She'd also known that, at this time of day, he always came alone.

No servants, no retinue.

As she waited for him in the center of the pond, barely

breathing (with her new, expanded lungs, barely breathing!), he came ever closer.

Then everything unfolded much as it had many times before. When he reached the edge of the pond, he rested, as he always did, on a stone structure. There he attended at length to himself: braiding and unbraiding his hands and legs, according to some cultural ritual.

Today, though, this ritual seemed more hurried, the motions of his hands and legs blurrier. As if he could not finish quickly enough. This time, his focus also appeared to be different; it was as if, this time, he were not looking at what he was *doing*, not really . . .

Today, he was looking at her.

Then, suddenly, he was no longer on the bench but rather gliding toward her. On his face, now clear, was the expression whose true nature it had been difficult to judge before, when she had watched him through a periscope. But now she could see that it *had* meant that.

He stopped just before her. "It's you," he whispered.

(It had meant that exactly!)

"Yes," she said.

Her voice worked too; she saw in his face that it did. And when he held out his hand to her, she understood that this was not only a gesture but also a question.

"Yes," she said.

Together, they glided. Together, they danced.

In his eyes, she saw that she had done everything right.

Then he was telling her that she was like someone from a dream. Then she was presenting to him the story she had prepared: that she was a princess in a nearby kingdom.

This, too, seemed to be right. Even the misleading parts were right.

Dreams.

His arms were around her. And she felt, as they moved together, that this world was hers as much as it was his.

"I have dreamed of you, too," she said. Then, suddenly, in a moment of delicious delirium, she was falling up to him and he was falling down to her, and it was love, love, love.

"Are you tired?" he asked, when their lips parted. She wasn't, of course. But she nodded anyway, a flutter in her stomach, and she glided with him to the side of the pond.

Here, he was solicitous with her, guiding her to "sit" (a new word) on the stone structure beside him.

She was even good at sitting.

He took her hand.

"Will you have dinner with me?" he asked. He gestured away, into the cold, clear distance, to the castle on the hill.

Did his beautiful world really extend so far?

"I want you to meet my parents," he said. "And I want . . . "

As he trailed away, she perceived the larger promise and a larger question, the thing that he wasn't quite saying, not yet.

In his eyes she could see it there, as if written.

"Yes," she said, to all of it.

His smile was radiant.

"Let's go now," he said. Then he looked away from her, down at himself, and he began the ritual she had noted before—the one that was always completed at the edge of the pond.

She looked at him carefully and sidelong, so that she might replicate it.

But something was odd. And she thought:

No amendments. No substitutions. No going back.

"I have always hated your family," the Witch had said.

The Prince, having completed his own ritual, gave her a concerned smile. "May I?" he asked, and she nodded reluctantly.

Kneeling before her, he proceeded to minister to her.

She swallowed.

She had, she thought, observed the people of this world so carefully. She'd thought that she'd understood.

And the Witch had never corrected her.

The Prince's hands had stopped moving, and now he was looking up at her strickenly.

"Your skates," he was saying. "I can't . . . "

She tried to meet his eyes. But she couldn't find a way to fix the way that he was looking at her, the utter bewilderment transitioning to . . .

Revulsion.

"What are you?" he whispered.
What a small thing to have gotten wrong.
And yet . . .
"They don't come off," she said.

Cures for Hiccups

1. Breathe: In. Out.

2. Breathe backwards: Out. In.

3. Retrieve a loved one from the underworld. But this time: Don't look back.

4. Retrieve a loved one from the underworld. But this time, really—really, really—don't look back.

5. *Don't look back!*

6. Rip out your throat, dramatically, as if you have made a discovery bearing upon some horrific transgression; rip out your throat, the way that Oedipus ripped out his eyes.

7. Both hiccup and do not hiccup.

8. Have sex with one of Oedipus' descendants. Afterwards, as you lie together, subtly guide the conversation toward this key revelation. Once you have persuaded your lover to state it, react as if this information were previously unknown to you ("You're related to *who*?!"), and that, now that you do know, this really changes everything.

9. Half hiccup, then one-third hiccup, then one-quarter hiccup, then one-fifth hiccup . . . until?

10. Get a friend to sneak up behind you and pop a balloon—*Bang!*

11. Get a friend to sneak up behind you and sketch the latest climate change predictions, together with a steep graph of rising

sea levels. Then, in a gray, hopeless tone, have your friend ask: "What now?"

12. Solve the Sphinx's riddle.

13. Get a friend to sneak up behind you and shoot you—*Bang!*

14. Say to the Sphinx, cannily, flirtily, and between hiccups: "I have a riddle for *you*."

15. Get mauled by the Sphinx.

16. Via DNA analysis, confirm that the person you are presently dating is really pretty distantly related to Oedipus. Then have sex with them—backwards.

17. Count to three.

18. Count to a million.

19. Retrieve a loved one from the underworld, backwards. But this time: Be sure to look back.

20. *Look back!*

21. Kiss a dragon, smoky and sweet—first kiss.

22. Kiss a dragon, toothy and tonguey and with third-degree burns—bad kiss.

23. Gargle lead.

24. Gargle arsenic.

25. Gargle mercury.

26. Gargle the periodic table.

27. Have sex with a dragon. (Good sex!)

28. Have dissatisfying sex with a dragon. Where the dragon comes way before you and then goes immediately to sleep, exhaling smoke as he snores. Then, as you hiccup, poke him questioningly ("Um . . . ?") between his bejeweled ribs. Finally, have him open one baleful, bleary eye, and say, "What?"

29. Get a friend to sneak up behind you and bring you back from the underworld (forwards or backwards).

30. Marry the good dragon.

31. Marry the bad dragon.

32. Visit the Oracle at Delphi. Then hiccup so violently that she cannot understand your question.

33. Get a friend to sneak up behind you and shoot you—backwards. *Gnab!*

34. Allow a vampire to turn you.

35. Turn a vampire to the Dark side.

36. Ask, quaveringly, of the Oracle at Delphi, "Are these the shadows of the things that Will be, or are they shadows of things that May be, only?"

37. Capture a Heffalump.

38. Retrieve Schrödinger's cat from the underworld. But this time: Don't open the box.

39. *Don't open the box!*

40. Get Christopher Robin to sneak up behind you and call you a "silly old bear."

41. Bewilder your hiccups with reverse psychology—That is what Tiggers do best.

42. Bewilder your hiccups with reverse psychology—backwards.

43. Invite Christoper Robin to a tea party.

44. Invite Christoper Robin to your 111th birthday party. As a prank, place the One Ring of Sauron on your finger and attempt to sneak away, while forgetting (somehow!) that invisibility is not going to render your persistent hiccups any less noticeable. And when (inevitably!) your hiccups out you anyway, have Christopher Robin waggle his finger reprovingly in your direction, then snatch you up playfully (if a little awkwardly; remember: he can't see you) and toss you into the air with a delighted laugh. Then, as you return to his arms—and as your plump, honey-filled tummy sloshes—have him call you a "silly old hobbit."

45. Use the Force.

46. Count all the grains of sand in all the beaches in all the world—backwards.

47. Fail to invite the Nazgûl to your 111th birthday party . . . then suffer the Nazgûl's curse.

48. Sleep for 100 years. That is what Tiggers do best.

49. Make out with Prince Charming, sweet and slow. Hiccup, kiss. Hiccup, kiss.

50. Make out with Prince Charming, fast. Hiccup. Tongue, tongue, tongue. Hiccup.

51. Rip out your malfunctioning, persistently hiccuping diaphragm and cast it into the depths of Mt. Doom, where it was forged.

52. Write an earnest letter to Santa Claus in which you explain that all you'd really like for Christmas this year is to stop hiccuping.

53. Summon the dead and exchange your malfunctioning, persistently hiccuping diaphragm for theirs. (But don't look back!)

54. Summon the Unborn and the Not-Yet-Conceived and exchange your malfunctioning, persistently hiccuping diaphragm for theirs. (But don't look forward!)

55. Summon the Never-Weres and the Never-Will-Bes and exchange your malfunctioning, persistently hiccuping diaphragm for theirs. (Don't look at all!)

56. Shoot your friend—*Bang!*

57. Divorce a dragon. That is what Tiggers do best.

58. Tell the hiccups that you are actually their father.

59. Tell the hiccups that you are actually Luke's father.

60. Open the Door to Narnia—hiccup bouts pass faster there.

61. Open the Door to Heaven to all those who believe in You—hiccup bouts (for so it is written) are less debilitating when they are shared.

62. Get a friend to sneak up behind you and tell your hiccups that they are actually Luke's father.

63. Inform your hiccups that your name is Inigo Montoya, and that they should prepare to die.

64. Write an earnest letter to the Oracle at Delphi in which you explain that all you'd really like for Christmas this year is to stop hiccuping.

65. Shoot a Heffalump—*Bang!*

66. Answer the Sphinx's newest riddle: What hiccups—on four legs, on two, on three? And what, whatever measures may be taken to alter its circumstances, never ceases to hiccup?

Say "Humankind," too quickly, too confidently.

Then, as the Sphinx smiles and backs you farther down the path (and as you beg for time), and as the cliff face crumbles beneath, fall and fall and then crash into the water and be drawn into the raging whirlpool of the terrible sea beneath. And as the Sphinx's distant smile fades forever from view, permit yourself to experience the sinking realization that the correct answer is far more specific than that—

It's you.

67. Hold your breath.

Our Entire Relationship is Ironic

We met at a campus party—a deeply ironic campus party—which didn't in the least seem to realize how ironic it was.

This was exactly what made it so ironic.

"Look at the irony on that side of the room," I said to you.

You, pointing, said, "Check out the irony over there."

"Pretty ironic," we agreed.

*

Many people have never even had ironic sex.

With others, the erotic eventually overshadows the irony, even when the act is initiated with the most ironic of intentions.

But for us?

"Ironic," you whispered in my ear, soft—that first time.

"Really fucking ironic," I agreed, a bit later.

*

The theme of our wedding was irony. No set colors, no special songs. Neither of us even bothered to inform the caterers, who prepared for us, nonetheless, as if on cue: watercress sandwiches.

God, that was ironic.

*

"This is going to be super ironic," I said, stroking my stomach. When, ironically, we decided to have children.

Twins?

Textbook irony.

*

"There's a lot of irony, going on in that room, right there," I observed, pointing to the nursery.

"It's spectacularly ironic," you agreed, as you emptied out the diaper genie.

*

Irony is famously difficult to define. But the third kid? That was probably the most ironic thing that ever happened to us.

The fourth kid, however—ironically enough—wasn't quite so ironic.

*

But they grew up. *Kids do that*, as we often had occasion to observe, with varying shades of irony.

And they were, we guessed, more-or-less ironic in doing this: ironic T-ball, ironic bake sales, ironic Suzuki.

But they didn't grow up as ironically as we grew up. Which—we both agreed—was pretty ironic.

*

Our first grandchild's career as a corporate lawyer? The second's as a bicycle mechanic?

Painfully ironic.

*

Your cardiac episodes, one after the other, each improbably coinciding with one of my knee replacement surgeries?

Yes.

*

But irony only thickens, as plots do. That's why they call it dramatic irony.

It's not just to be ironic.

And everything that presumably lies ahead of us? Ironic dementia, ironic incontinence? Our two pairs of gnarled hands, laid one against the other, palm to palm, with a slow, deliberate irony, for the very last time?

I can only imagine that that, too, will be almost unbearably ironic.

So, you know: looking forward.

Hybrid Bible

"Everything is to be created," said the Snake.

*

There was a great flood. In the violent rush, the Great Tower fell. At the same time, the One Language, which had been enshrined in the Tower's central citadel, was swept away. Over 40 days and 40 nights, the One was dissolved into many: all the tongues of the world.

*

"Everything is to be evil," said the Tree.

*

As the waters receded, new structures—ribs—were revealed, prominent in the shallows. As the world dried, these ribs did too; as they continued to dry, they acquired blood and flesh and the breath of life; from *these*, once the water had receded still farther, arose men.

And from men came Jacob.

*

"But also . . . " suggested the Woman.

*

The flocks of the King of Heaven consisted of hot, gaseous beasts who roamed nebulously through the Fields of the Night.

For seven years, Jacob tended to them.

At the end of this period, Jacob earned the loveliest of the King of Heaven's daughters, Mary, as his wife.

In the sky, she sparkled; her aura was red.

*

"Everyone is to have a Golden Calf," said Aaron.

*

But Mary was not enough.

So Jacob went on to earn Elizabeth, another of the King's daughters, who was nearly so lovely. Her aura was yellow.

But Elizabeth . . .

*

"Everyone is to have a Stone Tablet," said Moses.

*

So Jacob worked to earn them all, all the star daughters of the King, whose auras were blue and orange and silver . . . As wives, he took them: Leah and Ruth and Hannah and Rachel and Deborah and Esther and Miriam and Eve and Sarah and Priscilla and Martha and Jehosheba and . . .

*

Through the water that remained, a Great Whale roamed, predatory and cruel. Opening its immense jaw, it swallowed Jonah whole.

But then Jonah killed it from the inside, cracking the interior of its brain case.

He used only a pebble.

He used only a sling.

*

Amid the ribs that the receding flood had revealed lay mud. From this mud came the Four Horsemen.

*

For Jacob, however, wives—even all the wives in the sky—were not enough.

(When have wives ever been enough?)

So Jacob began to wrestle Angels.

*

The first Horseman, Pestilence, married the Lepers.

*

During his childhood and young adulthood, Samson had never

been positioned on the planks of a cross, then had nails riven through his hands and feet.

Not once, not in all of his many interactions with the Romans, had this ever happened to Samson.

It was a great secret, this non-Crucifixion.

It was also the source of Samson's great strength.

*

Jacob wrestled mightily with many Angels.

*

With this secret, Samson seemed destined to defeat the Philistines and free his people.

*

He wrestled with the Angel Leprosy and the Angel Pharaoh and the Angel Water Turning to Blood and the Angel Manna and the Angel Frogs and the Angel Ashes to Ashes and the Angel Lice and the Angel Livestock Plague and the Angel Dust to Dust and the Angel Boils and the Angel Hail and the Angel Forbidden Fruit and the Angel Locusts and the Angel Brother's Keeper and the Angel Darkness and the Angel Killing of Firstborn Children.

*

But then Samson's lover, Judas, betrayed him.

*

And then Jonah, whale-killer, gave names to all the remaining animals.

*

"Judas!" cried Samson, as the nails penetrated his hands and his feet.

*

After naming the animals, Jonah further exercised his ownership over them by skinning them, removing—variously—their feathers, pelts, and scales. With these pieces, he assembled a beautiful raft—a Raft of Many Colors.

*

Through these holes, Samson's fabled strength drained away.

*

And Jacob wrestled . . .

*

After his crucifixion, Samson was very weak—so weak that he was unable to roll away the stone that blocked his tomb.

*

The second Horseman, Famine, married the Giants.
   The third, War, married the Light of the World.

*

So Jacob, enraged, wrestled Judas, too, though Judas was not an Angel.
   "No one betrays Samson," said Jacob into Judas' ear.

*

And then Jonah, whale-killer, animal-namer, raft-maker, walked on water.

*

But Death, the fourth and most terrible of the Horsemen, married Lazarus.

*

Then Jonah, whale-killer, animal-namer, raft-maker, water-walker, spoke to the Burning Bush.

*

"Frankincense," said the Raft of Many Colors.
   "Myrrh," the Burning Bush.

*

"No one betrays Samson," Jacob repeated.

*

"Everyone is to be killed," said the Stone Tablet.

"Everyone is to be Resurrected," said the Golden Calf.

*

At the Horsemen's weddings, the blood of every guest became wine.
  (And then all the wine became water.)
  ((But then all the water become blood.))
  (((So, in the end, everyone was all right.)))

*

"Never," said Death.
  "Always," agreed Lazarus.

*

"I will wrestle all the fallen Angels," offered Jacob, by way of a wedding present.

*

"Everything is to end," said the Snake.

*

So there was a Second Great Event, an Anti-Flood. As all the waters of the world—Whoosh!—returned to Heaven, the Tower was restored and the One Language was reassembled and returned to the central citadel. Then all of Jacob's wives, in the many parts of the sky, could again perceive their Father's voice. All that time, over all those many years, He had been calling to them in the One Language, entreating them to return to Him.

*

"End drunkenly," said the Golden Calf.

*

As the waters were withdrawn, the post-Crucifixion stone was also swept away.
  Through the tomb's entrance (at last! at last!), Jacob rushed, his breath—and his veins—still foggy from what had occurred at the weddings. Here, he cradled what remained of his beloved.

*

"End luminously," said the Stone Tablet.

*

"Father, we come!" answered the stars: Mary, Elizabeth, Leah, Ruth, Hannah, Rachel, Deborah, Esther, Miriam, Eve, Sarah, Priscilla, Martha, Jehosheba and all the rest, in the One Language.

On Jonah's Raft of Many Colors they ascended, borne up by the waters. Each sparkled with her own aura: red, white, orange, silver, yellow, blue . . .

Beneath them, in comparison, even Jonah's Raft seemed pale and unremarkable.

*

"Everything is to go on living forever," said the Woman.

*

Over Samson's bones, Jacob wept.
He wept
in wine.
He wept
in water.
He wept
in blood.

*

"And be destroyed," said Aaron.

*

Jonah, whale-killer, animal-namer, raft-maker, water-walker, Burning Bush-speaker, weighted with the authority of his many accomplishments, said to the others of Jacob: "Let him be. *Let Jacob be.*"

So they let Jacob be.

*

"And eternally ascend," said the Raft of Many Colors.

*

Up, up, up, in a coach made from the bones of the Great Whale that Jonah had defeated, went the Horsemen and their marriage partners, and all the Angels with whom Jacob had ever wrestled (for the King of Heaven would welcome them, too), and Samson's bones—for Jonah, who knew what was best for Jacob, took these bones firmly away from Jacob.

*

"And be redeemed," said the Tree.

*

Carrying these bones, Jonah took his own seat inside the coach—the seat of greatest honor—beneath the reconstructed fragments of the skull that he had long ago shattered, using only a pebble, using only a sling.

"Let Jacob be," Jonah repeated, as the coach went higher.

*

"End in sand," said Moses.

*

Everything (nearly everything), everywhere (nearly everywhere), was drawn up into the sky: waters, stars, people, Horsemen, coaches, and bones.

The world beneath was left dry and empty.

In the resulting desert, only two living figures remained: only Judas, only Jacob.

Two together, wrestling.

*

"End in fire," said the Burning Bush.

*

"No one betrays Samson," Jacob repeated.

The Anatomy of a Dream, Part 4 (Or: 5 More Reasons)

1. For centuries, great thinkers have devoted themselves to nebulous aims: making people healthy, making people happy. Even making them "ethical."

They keep failing.

But it is imperative, it is clear to you (for you are, in your own quiet, hidden way, a great thinker) to set research goals that are narrow, concrete, and actionable. As in:

- Dolphin-parsnips
- Alligator-onions
- Orangutan-cucumbers

2. THAT is a checklist.

3. Once such a list has been agreed upon, it will become possible (then and only then) to begin to strike off component items, line by line, by sequentially and methodically achieving them.

4. Check?

5. Check.

Rock, Paper, Scissors

The first animal belonged to the sky. Its edges were perfectly straight and its corners were square.

Long vessels striped the animal's thin white body, spaced in horizontal rows. They carried a light blue blood.

On the animal's lower surface, just left of center, protruded the small bulge of an early pregnancy.

Now, eager to hunt, the animal descended. Along its body's central crease, it flattened and refolded its wings.

Sweeping low over the savanna, the animal perceived a flash of reflected light, partly hidden by the grass. In response, it re-angled its wings, intending to return to the sky.

Too late.

From the grass, two blades ascended. As they swung closed, they caught the animal along its crease, severing it into two sheets.

Snip!

From one edge of the severed tissue, the animal's fetus slipped out, like a letter from an envelope. In the air, as it fell, the fetus quivered briefly. But soon it was still.

*

The blades belonged to a second animal. When these blades (as now) were extended horizontally, they served as a set of sharp jaws.

Over its dead prey, the second animal snapped these jaws, over and over. To execute each snap, it pressed together a pair of metal loops, which presently served as its skull.

With each snap, the animal created a new flurry of confetti. Down the animal's blades these pieces fluttered, toward a mouth located at the blades' intersection; this orifice was bordered by a hinge.

Often, the animal's meals was leisurely. Today, however, just as it began to eat, it perceived a *Thump!*, which was followed by a low rumble.

Flee!

Nimble in its panic, the animal upended itself. In this new configuration, its appendages took on new functions. Its jaws became its legs and the metal loops became its hips.

Abandoning its kill, the animal set off in a seesawing gallop. First, it compressed its hips, then it split them apart. Compressed them, then split them apart. Compressed, then split apart. Compressed . . .

Behind it, the rumble became louder.

The animal galloped, clack, clack, clack.

Louder closer louder.

The attacker threw the animal to the ground

Smash!

then rolled all the way over it.

Crunch!

Twitchily, the animal tried to pull its appendages apart, desperate to use them, either as legs or as jaws. But they were too badly dented.

The attacker rolled over the animal again, this time from the opposite direction (*Crunch!*). And again, from the original direction. (*Crunch!*)

And again.

Crunch!

And again.

Crunch!

And again.

Crunch!

Out of the splintered loops of the animal's pelvis-skull, its brain oozed, bloody and molten.

*

The third animal was immense and gray. It was also a perfect sphere—no head and no limbs. Sense organs, embedded into tiny pits, dotted its skin.

Positioned above its prey, the animal opened its lips. Stone scraped against stone. With deeper, grinding sound, it everted its stomach.

Inside, flakes of quartz bristled, diamond hard. With these flakes, the animal abraded its prey into glittering flecks.

Sparks flew.

As the animal worked, it perceived a small shadow. Then a *Swish!* and a soft *Puff!*, as two tiny feet landed on its hull.

Frantically, the animal began pumping its abdominal muscles, initiating the maneuvers that would be required to retract its stomach, regularize its outer surface, and launch into a defensive roll.

Before it could finish, it perceived something ominous.

A tickle.

Fibers snaked into one of the pits that dotted the animal's skin. Through these fibers, a burning venom was injected.

At the jolt of it, the animal managed a small, abortive lurch.

But as the venom spread, the animal began to become stiffer. And stiffer stiffer stiffer. Then, with a final, grinding beat, its insides became hard—as hard as its outer hull—and its heart stopped.

*

The fourth animal, like the first, was white and thin.

From its prey, the animal retracted a pair of injection fibers; these fibers were connected to one of the horizontal lines of its venomous blue blood.

Under other circumstances, the animal would have found this moment deeply satisfying.

This had been a good kill.

Just that morning, however, the animal's mate had been hunted and eaten, together with their unborn offspring.

What the animal experienced now was not exactly grief. What it felt, rather, was loss: profound and irremediable. Everything that the animal had already invested: all of the time and energy it had devoted to wooing, to fighting off other rivals, to the acrobatics of in-flight copulation . . . all of that had come to nothing.

Now, it would have to start over.

This late in the season, this effort would be desperate. What mates remained would be profoundly imperfect: creatures with asymmetric wings, misfolded edges, or rips in their skin.

But the animal had to try.

To survive the nuptial flight, it would require fuel. To answer that need, it had hunted. Now, to complete the harvest, it extruded a rectangular tongue coated in a corrosive digestive liquid.

Then it licked and it licked—resignedly and hopelessly, but nonetheless implacably—its saliva potent enough to dissolve the stone.

Three Pigs, One Wish

1.

"Wolf!" cried the little pig, "Let me come in!"

This time, it was not the door of a cottage in storybook land that separated them but rather the door of an apartment in 1908 Vienna.

The pig, in addition, was not precisely a pig. In one sense, she was a paper construct; on her surface, the parameters of her existence had been encoded in ink. Above that ink, a layer of additional misdirection had been dusted, which made her seem mostly human.

Similarly, the Wolf, somewhere behind that door, was not precisely a wolf. Not to every way of thinking. In another sense, he was a young man, brooding and pitiable, and not yet nineteen.

But the pig did not think in terms of these qualifiers.

Only in story.

And this story—the new story; the amended and inverted story—was written into her skin.

Instructions, in her skin.

("Let me come in!" she oink-snarled, and rapped at the door with her hooves.)

Urgency and imminence.

In her skin.

("Let me come in!" she huffed and puffed.)

The Imperative, in her skin.

("Let me come in!")

. . . And then the Wolf opened the door, just a little . . .

Through the slit, their eyes met . . . one wolfy eye first, then a second, as he let the door swing wider . . . and the Wolf drew in his own breath.

For he sensed—for so, inexorably, ran the text of the story—that there was something about her . . .

. . . something *striking* . . .

"

(And what, he thought, anyway—what, he thought, breathlessly—does a wolf have to fear from a pig?)

So the Wolf let her in.

Hours before, on a road outside the city, the pig had retrieved a bundle of yellow-white fibers from the ground; these fibers had fallen from a bale of straw on a cart. Now, forcing the Wolf to the floor, she held these fibers hard against his throat.

"Warum?" the Wolf wondered.

("Because you are the Wolf!")

Then she pulled back harder.

(In her skin her skin)

And harder and harder, so that she felt his face change, his eyes bulge, his skin give, then harder harder harder.

. . . *warum* . . . ?" he rasped, in a voice like ash.

Harder, *Because you are the Wolf!*, until there was blood on the straw. Harder, harder, harder, harder, *Because you are the Wolf!*, and his head came off in her hands, and she let go of it and of the bloody body too. In her own skin, she perceived cosmic convulsions, emanating from this moment and this place: the future altering as a result of what she had done.

A beginning to a different story . . .

(in her skin in her skin)

. . . its middle . . .

(in her skin in her skin)

The End.

Her ink bubbled and her paper smoldered. It was a delirious epilogue. In the heat of it, she danced. Danced upon the corpse, hoof by hoof by hoof by hoof, while the ripples of her action vibrated against her paper: the epic tragedy that she had prevented; all of the violence and inhumanity that would now not occur.

She danced until what remained at her feet was only a jelly, a *stain*. Then she spat, Oink, Oink, into the smear of it: the gore and shattered bones.

Beautiful.

The world spun. Even after breaking off her dancing, it continued to spin: around and around, driven by the ripples, which were immense and lovely. Uneasily, dizzily, she wondered . . .

Was it time to go?

Swish, whirl, blur.

She dabbed away the blood (most of it). She extinguished the smolder (most of it). She rearranged her hat and overcoat.

Perhaps—it was true—the hooves that doubled as her shoes were not entirely clean. And perhaps, here and there, just in small places, she was still on fire.

What did that matter?

But when the pig stumbled out of the apartment, slamming the door behind her, she felt . . .

. . . other ripples . . .

Coming up that hallway, just a few feet away, was . . . and here the pig snatched clumsily amid the ripples in order to find out who . . .

. . . the Wolf's roommate . . .

. . . August Kubizek . . .

Close to August, there were also ripples. These ripples were tiny (so what did they matter?).

((If they had not been standing together in the same hallway, she likely never would have sensed them!))

But these were not happy ripples.

August would be convicted for the Wolf's murder. There would be no other suspects. In the weeks before his execution, he would brood on the injustice of it. What would occupy him more, however, would be the visceral memory of what lay behind this door and the violent—seemingly senseless—loss of his friend.

For just a moment, the pig felt a little cold.

She shuffled her legs, her feet-hooves tangling; it was almost a curtsy. Then, with an awkward little hop, she pressed her snout against August's cheek (not quite a kiss, not really), for whatever comfort, anyway, that could ever be worth.

"Entschuldigung," she said.

August was unnerved. Astonished. Bewitched. As she pulled away, he remained motionless, heart beating fast. He *wanted* to say something. To ask who she was. To ask her to stay.

But the words didn't come.

The pig fled the building, then out into the streets.

Outside Vienna, she kicked off her disguise. Without it, she went faster. Then faster. (And faster.) Once she had attained an improbable speed, she grunted softly, then slipped into a space that—to a certain way of thinking—wasn't there, into a forest where no person had ever been, where the sun rose in the west and set in the east and where the great oaks shrank, shrank, down to saplings and smaller still, and were swallowed up entirely by soil, then ceased to be.

"Chinny-chin-chin!" she sang.

2.

What the first little pig had done would have served happily enough. But the same text was printed in the skin of the second little pig, who was cleverer than the first. When her turn came, she entered the same forest. But she went more deeply than her sister had. When she emerged, it was earlier and farther west: a night in late autumn, 1888, close to a town, Braunau am Inn.

In the darkness, in a strand of trees on the town's outskirts, the pig smelled something—exactly the scent she had primed herself for.

A rot that grew on wood.

Dilating her nostrils, the pig hunted it down, sniffing and trotting over the damp ground. There, inside a stump . . .

Yes.

Reconfiguring herself in the form of a woman, the pig collected the rot, then slipped into the center of the sleeping town.

Forcing the door of the Apotheke, the pig gathered the required reagents and equipment, then assembled a distillation apparatus.

After suspending the rot in one of these liquids, the pig passed it through the apparatus. She heated and cooled it. Afterwards, she heated and cooled *this* fraction. Then again. And again.

Once the final layer of liquid had evaporated, what remained was a cluster of potent crystals, glittering pink under the rays of the pig's candle.

An abortifacient.

In the morning, the pig purchased meat, vegetables, spices and cooking equipment at the town market. Retreating again to the town outskirts, she chopped and stirred over a wood-fed fire.

In the afternoon, the pig adjusted her aura. Plausibly arrayed as a cook, she slipped into the Wirtshaus—an establishment to which the Wolf's mother would occasionally (and today in particular) come for lunch.

At her table, bowing, the pig presented the soup she had prepared.

Once again, there were ripples everywhere. Nearly all of them were exquisite. Cataclysmic. And yet . . .

. . . and here the pig flinched . . .

And yet . . .

The ripples that surrounded Klara were not like that.

This time, the pig knew, the blood (in her skin in her skin in her skin) would be different. It would be intimate and localized. It would emerge secretly, clot by clot.

Klara had already lost three children. Tomorrow, when the cramping started, she would try to push the pieces back into herself.

Wasn't she simply disgusting?, her husband would ask, louring over her as she wept. Hadn't she always been disgusting?

"Entschuldigung," murmured the pig now. She tried to keep her tone light, as if to assign her regret to something trivial: something about the way the table was set.

Klara look up at her sharply.

The pig, though, kept her eyes mild and dark: meeting her gaze, even as she did not quite meet it.

Strange . . . But didn't the soup smell good?

With a tentative smile, Klara dismissed the pig. Then she lifted her spoon.

She was *quite* hungry, after all. For weeks—between, at least, the bouts of nausea—she had been *so* hungry.

As she ate, she did notice a curious seasoning. But didn't everything taste a little different now? Feel a little different? And wasn't that wonderful?

The pig slipped away. As she left through a side door, the Wirthaus' proprietor shot her a suspicious look. But the pig was already going very quickly, carried along by the momentous ripples that she had generated: the abductions, murders, and cruelty she had prevented; the great tragedy that she had unmade.

The Wirtshaus' proprietor, in comparison, was stout and slow. He decided not to follow.

Where the town ended, the pig dropped to four legs. On and on she ran, until she reentered the forest of the shrinking trees, where her sister was, or had gone, or would be. Under their leaves she raced: leaves, which, in a certain sense, were not there; leaves through which a strange wind whispered; leaves that contracted, smaller and smaller, until they became juvenile nubs, and their stems began to absorb them.

"Chinny-chin-chin!" she sang.

3.

What either of her sisters had done would have served happily enough. But there was a third little pig, cleverer still. In her skin was written the same imperative.

From the backwards forest, where the greenery receded, this pig emerged a few months earlier than the second had, on a warm evening in mid-August, 1888.

Inside Braunau am Inn, she entered the crumbling wreck of an abandoned house, where she found a small dense object—a brick.

It was perfect.

Walking elegantly on two legs, the pig carried the brick to a spot closer to the center of the town, to a place where the pedestrian portion of the street was poorly maintained. She sought out one large crack in particular.

The brick, the pig confirmed, fit inside this crack almost exactly. Just one corner protruded . . .

Perfect.

The pig pressed herself casually against the neighboring wall. She did not have to wait long.

Within moments, a man barreled around the corner.

The Wolf's father.

Lost in thoughts of a mounting urgency, Alois caught his foot on the tip of the brick. He would have tripped, except . . .

Stepping forward, the pig offered Alois what appeared to be an arm. "Entschuldigung," she murmured.

Alois was startled. And embarrassed. And confused.

Had this woman seen him stumble? Or had she, too, been walking quickly? Did she believe she had bumped into him?

Finally, Alois gave the pig a brisk nod—a gesture that (he felt) constituted exactly the right compromise between thanks and blame.

Then he shrugged her away.

Again, there were ripples. This pig, the cleverest of them all, perceived them with perfect clarity.

The collision had jostled, just slightly, the entire lower half of Alois' body. Including—critically—his testicles.

As Alois continued toward home, he would return to the pressing thoughts that had occupied him before the collision.

At home would be Klara.

In Klara, Alois would release the semen that had been jostled by the stumble. This time, a particular sperm, its position altered, would emerge a few beats earlier. This time, it would swim into the left tube, not the right. When it reached the top, what it had hoped to encounter would not be there.

Then this sperm would die.

(in her skin in her skin in her skin)

In parallel, another sperm, its timing also altered, would enter the right tube. Here, it would encounter an egg—*the* egg (the only egg that this was ever about)—and initiate, this time, another kind of child:

A daughter.

This daughter would be neither exceptionally good or exceptionally bad. She would live competently and unremarkably: temperamental, perhaps, but never destructive. (And always—for this, at least, might ever be said of her— devoted to her mother.)

Then history would forget her.

Now, as Alois strode irritably away, the pig removed the brick from the street. Walking nimbly among the ripples (The End, The End, *The End*), she returned to the abandoned house, where she returned the brick to its original location.

Outside the house, she let her costume fall, then her front legs.

On four legs, she went faster. And faster faster. Then, she entered that wood that wasn't, where the leaves leaped abruptly from the ground before spiraling upwards, elegant and slow, and adhering to the branches, where their autumnal colors were diluted, gradually and beautifully, into green.

"Chinny-chin-chin," she sang.

0.

For years, the girl had amused her mother and sisters with her storybook magic, persuading the ducklings in the pond to mature into beautiful swans and the fish, "for love," to grow legs and come to land. And the dog to sleep for days, under the influence of a "curse," until her first sister, Abigail, kissed it awake. And a frog (after her second sister, Adina, kissed it) to lurch about self-importantly, hilariously pantomiming the actions of a prince.

Later, in the prison camp, she had retained the storybook—retained it, somehow, even when everything else had been taken.

Like her family.

Smoke. *Smoke.* In her own head, the girl could pretend that that wasn't what it was. Not her mother. Not her sisters. That in reality the story had gone the way it was supposed to go: that, from the gingerbread house, they had gotten out (gotten out the right way), and into the forest they had raced, and it was only the *witch* that had gone out *that way*. It was only the witch that . . .

No.

But she had her storybook.

("Seven-league boots," her mother had urged when the men had first come.

"Beanstalk," insisted Abigail on the train.

"Magic porridge pot," whispered Adina after their mother and Abigail were gone.)

But she couldn't do it: couldn't do it then, couldn't do any of it, couldn't do anything, even when they had begged her to.

Couldn't feel it (no play no play no play).

Couldn't find it (no play).

Couldn't feel.

Afterwards, when they were no longer there to beg her, there seemed to be no story in the book that could ever return things to the way they needed to be.

Smoke, collecting out of the sky.

Smoke, becoming a person.

Backwards smoke.

ekomS, ekomS.

That was not a story; there was no such story.

But it was a dream.

When she slept, she began to see it: a tangled forest composed of subsiding branches and shrinking trunks.

During the day: Hunger hunger hunger.

At night, when she slept, she could see it.

During the day: Hunger work cold hunger.

At night, while she slept, she tried to find a way into the trees.

During the day: Hunger. Nothing left. Hunger.

At night, she kept failing.

She knew how to fix it, if she could only get in. She knew, because she had paid attention before, who to target. *Who.* So she began to speak it—the name, the who—high and breathy and backwards and only to herself.

How to unmake . . .

. . . and by unmaking, to remake . . .

(She sensed, more and more, that this—Unmaking—was what real magic was.

Serious magic. Not play.)

If she could get in.

While she slept, she also held the storybook close (which still no one had taken from her, and this continued to *prove* the persistence of her magic, even as she could perform no other kind), and sometimes, though she could not enter, she could feel parts of the pages moving away from her, parts of the pages entering, and . . .

The pages could get in.

The pages!

Yes yes yes.

So she made Jack first (hadn't Abigail wanted a beanstalk? hadn't Abigail insisted that she try?). She ripped out the first page from Jack's story, folded him out of it, and wrote instructions on his skin.

"Kill the Ogre!"

But the first Jack could find no way within those trees. (No path! he said, with his paper-flesh lips. No path! he said, while every part of him trembled.)

She unfolded him, this failed Jack, and then remade him. This time she wrote the words in deeper. This time she folded him harder.

This time he did not come back.

So she made another Jack—and another—until all the pages in this story were gone. Then the Billy Goats Gruff, 1, 2, 3. "Kill the Troll! Kill the Troll! Kill the Troll!"

Then a score of other champions, until she had no more ink. Afterwards, she began to use mud, which she mixed with some of her own blood. (Though what did she have inside of herself, anymore? What blood could she spare?)

But most of her golems did not come back at all, and the rest returned sadly (The forest was too tangled, they said. The forest was too strange!), until the storybook was in tatters, most of the pages gone, and what remained were . . .

. . . Pigs?

Pigs, who were backwards creatures, even before she made them into golems ("Kill the Wolf! Kill the Wolf! Kill the Wolf!"). Beings without category, who had hooves but who chewed no cud.

After she sent them away, she could see them, but only dimly, receding and receding, in a smear of trees . . .

. . . and in the night, as she slept, they came back again. When she opened her eyes, they pressed their paper flesh snouts against her hands and softly oinked their reports to her.

Time a Upon Once.

She held them close, smoothing them to her like blankets. They, too, pressed themselves closer, flattening themselves against her and against the storybook.

As she closed her eyes again (so tired, always tired!), she felt their inks lift and the inks' pigments unmix, and return, in part, to her: blood of her blood.

Because that is what Unmaking means.

To wake up, to wake up . . .

. . . warm and elsewhere, in a bed that was not hers . . . and yet it was.

No golems. No paper.

(Only the storybook, clean and whole.)

But a sound of voices—of laughter—in another room. And a glimpse of a calendar, across the room: familiar and yet also not familiar, and the view from the window of the falling snow.

A winter—another sort of winter—in 1944.

Feet in the hallway, a knock on the door, Abigail shouting, Adina in a teasing singsong, and her mother, with equal, though more sedate affection:

Sleepyhead! Sleepyhead!

Didn't she want breakfast this morning?

And hadn't she slept long enough?

And there was another moment, just one more moment, after that, as she pushed back the covers, her bare feet on the rug . . . and a final flutter, as the magic settled, and the gulf closed, and the imperatives of the new reality set in . . . and for a moment, just one for moment, though the memory itself had faded, the faintest intimation of what it meant remained, flickering in her head and in her heart: an immense and incomprehensible happiness.

Hamlet in Midsummer

The poison merchant was classically Greek—a creature out of place and out of time. During the sale, he had chittered on and on in heavily accented Danish. Something about "a little western flower."

Before the contest, one blade was secretly anointed. The other remained clean. But as the two combatants fenced, each briefly disarmed the other. In the resulting confusion, they exchanged their weapons and continued sparring with the swapped swords.

The anointed blade cut them both.

As the poison began to burn, the first combatant confessed what he had done. "We are both doomed," he said. "Please forgive me."

Sword to sword, they sank to the floor.

But they did not die.

Instead, as they lay tangled, eye to eye, heart to heart, they experienced something else.

"Hamlet?" asked the first, who had sustained the deeper cut. "Hamlet?" he repeated, a little softer, as he reached out, trembling, to brush the hair from the other's forehead.

For Hamlet, whose wound was not so deep, the effect of the potion was briefly delayed. But at his adversary's touch—for so it began—he experienced a brief, strange flash of a woman's face. This face was pale and wet and framed by flowers.

Then he blinked.

In that moment, and in every moment after, there was only one face—only one face in all the world—and the older one was forgotten.

"Laertes," he whispered.

4 and 20 Dead Cats

"A pie!" cried King Schrödinger, opening the box.

With a dazed smile, he accepted the utensils I offered.

"An odd flavor," he said, chewing. So I explained.

"A cat!" he snorted, wiping his lips on his sleeve. "But why is it not *moving*?"

*

But kings are busy men.

With a shake of his head—gentle, apologetic, but also imperious—King Schrödinger declined my gift.

*

"Should I open it?" King Schrödinger asked. Eyes to mine: a spark.

But he was not to be my lover.

*

Or my friend.

*

"The cat is dead, your Majesty," I said.

"What is 'dead'?" asked the king.

*

"I feel no need of food, just now," he said. "I'm not . . ." and here he gestured emptily, as if struggling for the word.

*

But then, in a wild moment of clarity, I thought, *I can't.*

Not this time.

So I snatched it away, pie and cat together, even though I risked offending him.

Even though kings feel entitled to presents, once they are offered.

*

" . . . hungry?" I said.

"What is 'hungry'?" he asked.

*

With the unopened box, I ran back to my ship, which still stood in the harbor.

*

When King Schrödinger burped, a small "Meow" escaped his lips.

*

And so, because the king wasn't hungry, he instead took me to his counting house.

"What a lot of money," I said.

*

"Delicious!" shouted King Schrödinger.

*

"Muh-Knee . . . " he said. Then he shrugged and smiled. With two hands, he cupped a pile of coins and threw them into the air. Most, with a bright clatter, returned to the table.

The rest, to his absolute unconcern, fell on the floor.

*

So I kissed him.

*

"I just call them shinies!" he said.

*

Once inside the ship, where my map was, I crossed out King Schrödinger's homeland, setting the usual "X" upon it, to mark what I had just done.

*

On my map, I crossed out King Schrödinger's homeland, like a lie.

To save it.
(For a while.)

*

Then the king pushed a pile of "shinies" in my direction.
   "You can play too!" he said.

*

On my map, I left King Schrödinger's homeland unmarked. Let another ship come, I thought. Let it not be mine.

*

"Try it!" he invited.

*

The king chewed thoughtfully at the forkful of crust and cat. "It's missing something," he said.

*

On my map, I left King Schrödinger's homeland unmarked. Let my incomplete bookkeeping be a bedevilment to everyone. At least I had done it.

*

"A pocketful of rye?" I suggested.

*

"I feel . . . " he began. He burped sourly, and his expression was unhappy. "I feel . . . "

*

"Pie is fine," said King Schrödinger, looking dubiously at the confection. "But I rather prefer music."

*

"Ill?" I asked him.

*

Music? So, while he ate, I sang for him, a Song of Sixpence.

*

"What is 'ill'?" he asked with an uneasy smile. Fork to his mouth—one more bite.

*

Melodically and euphoniously.

*

Turbulently and tragically.

*

"I do not particularly like cats," he admitted, and twisted his lips a little. "They make me . . . " He held up one finger, as if to mark the thought. Then he convulsed daintily into a handkerchief.

*

So, because he had shown me his counting house, I showed him my ship.

*

". . . sneeze?" I suggested.

*

"That was *lovely*, maid," he said to me. In his eyes was a familiar gleam. "It fills me with . . . a *feeling*," he said. "I haven't the *word*, but . . .

*

A Song of Sixpence, my king, to aid your digestion.

*

"Hope?" I suggested, a little savagely.

*

From the crust, a cat's head partially protruded: the ears, the top half of the whiskers, and the tip of the nose.

"Kitty!" he shouted.

*

"This is an odd ship you have," said King Schrödinger unsteadily. "Does it even . . . float?"

*

He ate the entire pie, including the short-haired calico that had been baked inside. Every crumb.

*

What I had just done settled in my throat: a familiar sickness. So I commanded my ship to leave: "Next destination!"

*

"A present?!" he cried, and clapped excitedly.

*

"You must come from . . . far away, maid," he said, furrowing his brow as he paced my ship. Then he swallowed.

*

"Tell me of your homeland, maid," said King Schrödinger, as we lay together on my ship.

*

"Tell me of your homeland, maid," said King Schrödinger, as we lay together in his counting house.

*

So I kissed him, again and again. I did it because something in me was still soft. I did it because something was still there.

*

"Next destination!"

*

I kissed him because I was empty. I did it to be cruel.

*

"This is not an entirely . . . pleasant ship," said King Schrödinger with a strained smile, as if embarrassed for me.

*

"My homeland!" I shouted. Then I laughed and laughed.

*

"I love you, maid," he said.

*

"My homeland is miserable," I whispered.

*

Because I wanted to show him.

*

"Misherbull?" King Schrödinger said, struggling with the syllables. "Is that a sort of cat?" he asked, teasing a bit of brindled tabby from out between his teeth.

*

Because I wanted him.

*

Because . . .

*

"Sorrowful," repeated the king thoughtfully. "Is that the cat's name?" he asked. Then he began to stroke the long-haired Siamese that purred within the circle of crust.

*

After coughing violently for several minutes, he disgorged a ball of hair into his hand.

*

"I like your throne!" he laughed, pointing to my pilot's chair.

*

The king gave it—then me—a distasteful look. As if he might have preferred feathers.

*

So, because King Schrödinger would not eat and because he would not open the box, I sang for him.

*

"Maid," he said, "I'm not sure that . . . "

*

Folding my hands, as a minstrel might, I recited the verses from the ancient Song of Sixpence: "These pies, O King, are baked in my homeland . . . "

*

" . . . I'm not sure that I *like* you."

*

"Where suffering is pressed into the very cats, the very ovens, the very food!"

*

"I like the window, too!" he said. Then, with a delighted giggle, he hopped over to the control panel and peered through the ship's viewing screen.

*

"We package them into boxes, O King."

*

He coughed and he coughed and he coughed and he coughed.

*

"And we load them onto ships, in search of Paradises."

*

"Paradise?" he asked with wide, clear, innocent eyes. Then he wiped a spray of whiskers from his mouth.

*

"Where nothing lasts, O King! And where we are always angry!"

*

Sweet eating, king.

*

"And we come through the gaps, all the bright gaps, between dimensions . . . "

*

Then brightly, while his lips trembled, he asked, "Are there any blackbirds in your homeland?"

*

" . . . We claw our way through the cracks, in order to share . . . "

*

"Paradise?" he asked, and took my hand.

*

"To share!" I cried.

*

"Leave my land, maid," King Schrödinger whispered.

*

"To share!"

*

But, for all his coughing, nothing ever came up.

*

"How many lands?" asked the king, as he stared at my map.

*

"4 and 20," I lied.

*

On his chin, there were wet crumbs. Around his lips, there was a little blood, from where a claw had scratched him, going in.

*

"How many?" he demanded.

*

"King Schrödinger," I said, "I have brought you a present."
   "Thank you," he smiled.

*

"4 and 220," I lied.

*

Then King Schrödinger summoned a servant, who carried the unopened box away, to one of the storage rooms in the basement of the palace.

*

"Across the universe, our ships manifest, again and again . . . "

*

Crazy king, I thought, as I watched the servant go.
   Maddening king.
   Would he really never open it?

*

" . . . We descend into lands like yours, in order to disseminate what we carry . . . "

*

"Maid," winked King Schrödinger, setting the box aside—another invitation. "My queen is in the parlour, eating bread and honey . . . "

*

" . . . To show you what we are!"

*

"And she will never know . . . "

*

Out of the crust, an orange tabby cat sprang and scratched off the king's nose.

*

Then I parted my robe, revealing what was beneath: all the lines, all the scars.

*

"It is called 'pain,'" I told him.

*

"It is called *age*," I rasped.

*

His pronunciation was improving. "Mu-ti-la-tion?" he repeated, while the blood poured down his face. "Dis-fi-gure-ment?"
    I smiled encouragingly.

*

"Cats . . . " sighed the king and set the box aside.

*

From his castle, high on the hill, we watched the fields of his kingdom, once vivid and lush, begin to become yellow.
    All of the crops were dying, I explained. All of the leaves were curling up.

*

"4 and 20 trillion," I said with an approximating shrug.

*

"What is that . . . color?" he asked.

*

Sometimes, as I descend from my ship, I think: *This* will be the time when I do not share my wares.

*

"Famine," I said.

*

Will it be this time?

*

Together, we looked out of the great window. Everywhere, on the roads that crisscrossed his kingdom, people were lying on the ground. Some were kicking weakly.

*

No.

*

And others, more vigorously . . .
　"They are 'fighting,'" I told the king.

*

Others were still.
　"It's called disease," I told him.

*

Yes.

*

He looked over at me, bewildered, as the sun went away.
　"Night," I whispered.

*

It would be impossible to explain what this was like: to emerge, with all these cats, from a place of heat and darkness, and to enter a place like *this*, where the brightness was unremitting and where people have never hurt.
　And to have nothing but—everything and—the inclination to share.

*

"Betrayal," I said.

*

"Cold," I told him, before he could ask.

*

To share . . .

*

"Who are you, maid?" he demanded.

*

To share! To share!

*

"I work at the bakery," I said—no answer at all.

*

"No one," I said.

*

From the throne room, I brushed the remaining crumbs through the open window.

The wind took them. Through the air, they tumbled, finely and minutely, diffusing into every corner of his kingdom.

*

And wasn't that a dainty dish to set before a king?

*

"My name is Pandora," I said.

The Anatomy of a Dream, Part 5 (Or: 6 More Reasons)

1. You already have a laboratory coat. You picked it out carefully. It is slick and crisp and white.

It also has a belt.

At that belt, you'll store your laboratory instruments, packaged into holsters.

Then, once you've positioned the targets that you would like to join—1 sea cucumber + 1 prairie vole—you'll whip out your laboratory stapler gun and shout: "Bam! Bam! Bam!"

2. There are better ways to have a unicorn. Better than a medieval paining. Better than a My Little Pony figurine.

A real horse + a real narwhal.

A real howhal, a real narse.

Real real real.

3. It is fun to design new drinks.

It is fun to drink them.

You're a mixologist at heart.

And, for you, Nature is just another liquor cabinet.

4. You cannot be cold when you share your blood with a polar bear. You cannot feel vulnerable when the plates of an armadillo compose you, serving as a second skin. And you cannot feel naked when the ringlets of a lion's mane, lustrous and tawny, emerge from your own follicles, curling ferociously—possessively—over what was exposed before.

Like a hot drink.

Like armor.

Like a royal gown.

5. This seems cool, all of this. And haven't you always wanted to be cool?

6. You struggle to sleep. It's as if, like the princess in the old story, there is something beneath your mattress . . .

Peas?

(Except there aren't.

You've checked.)

Pea-watermelons?

(No.

You've double-checked.)

What you need, you increasingly realize, is something that, while you sleep, will be *soft enough*.

Something that, when you cuddle with it, will not merely offset all disturbances but actively protect you from them. (Or preemptively annihilate them). ((Or . . .))

You know what you need, anyway.

You do.

But the softness you are craving exceeds the softness of any animal that presently exists.

It will, you know, be necessary to make something new. To combine, in particular, the cuddliest characteristics of animals that have fur and animals that have no bones.

Mammals + invertebrates.

Outside, your creation will be fluffy, like a kitten. Inside, it will be equally cuddly: squishy, like a snail.

The exterior of a fox, the interior of an oyster.

Chinchilla fur, wrapped about a jellyfish.

The correct part of a rabbit, the correct part of a worm.

Each a pillow, each a night companion.

Soft, soft, soft.

Sinking in, close to each, soothed by the (also soft) sounds of their hybrid hearts, you might at last be able to sleep.

(Finally, finally.)

(Finally, soft.)

Because, before this, you have never slept, not really.

Only dreamed.

Strip Poker

I have lost every hand, until now.

All my clothes are gone, because I threw them in. Then my skin. Then my bones.

Organ after organ.

My brain in a wet splat.

You smirk at me from across the table.

You have your own eyes, and you have mine too, somewhere in that pile of clothes and flesh.

But for all of that, you cannot see what I have.

These cards. *This* time.

As you continue smirking, I toss down my heart. It thumps between us, hot and bright.

"All in."

The Comma:
With Her, Bear Is Savage

If a bee larva is raised on royal jelly, it will become a queen; if an alligator embryo is incubated at a low temperature, it will become female; if an Acrididae insect matures under crowded conditions, it will become a locust.

Otherwise, each will develop in another way, to become (respectively) a worker bee, a male, and a plain old grasshopper.

This is called developmental plasticity.

Among the bears that our lab studied, something similar appeared to be operating. They too could develop in one of two ways. Recently, however, the frequency of the rarer morphotype had been increasing, to the detriment of the human populations that bordered its habitat.

Our lab was determined to find out why.

We worked in the tradition of the nineteenth-century physician John Snow, who had traced a cholera epidemic to a contaminated well. Like him, we created a map.

To which section of the forest, we wanted to know, were these irregular bears native? Where had they been born? And—most importantly—where had the bear mothers been when, as embryos, these profoundly destructive morphotypes had been gestating inside of them?

To get answers, we studied the statements of survivors collected at the site of each incident. From which direction, each survivor had been asked, had the bear come? Where had it gone afterwards?

We also reviewed decades of data collected by field biologists. Who, we wanted to know, were the affected bears' parents? What was their territory?

Everything we learned we added to our map.

Most of the time, the site of a given incident could only be imperfectly traced to the site of a bear's gestation. In many cases, *years*, many years, passed between the bear's embryonic period and the first documented event of morphotype-defining behavior. During these years, additional factors might blur the trail; of these, migrations were both the most common and the most confounding.

By integrating all of these data, however, we were able to build a map with many circles. *Clustered* circles.

Our answer, like John Snow's answer, seemed to be water.

The Y. River.

In particular: the frequency of the destructive morphotype was highest along one five-mile section. Even more particularly, it occurred most frequently in the most upstream portion of this section; overall, our data were consistent with a model in which a causative agent had been introduced to the Y. River at a single point, then progressively diluted as the water carried it downstream.

And at the top of this implicated stretch, its security fence close to the bank, its efflux pipe opening directly into the water? A factory.

*

Expedited Editorial Services (EES) processed thousands of manuscripts a week. It would edit your manuscript "fast," boasted a brochure that Ling and A.J. brought to one of our lab meetings. It would do it "cheap."

To this same meeting, Mei and Alec brought photos. Most were of the front of the EES building; several showed the company's title etched on the front doors. Only two, much grainier than the rest, showed the back side of the factory, which faced the Y. River.

Could Mei and Alec get us a better picture?

All of *these* pictures, Mei explained, had been taken from the public record. No one was going to let us drive through there. Certainly not with cameras.

Okay.

Michel reported that he had called EES. But the line—they'd said—was for customers only. So unless Michel wished to place an order . . . ?

Flustered, Michel had gone on to describe a not terribly

plausible scenario, and why it would necessitate the following order . . .

EES had hung up on him.

Mei snorted. This was exactly, she said, why Michel had never succeeded as a spy but had instead been forced to go into science.

"*I* think you're a spy," said Fenhua, laying a comforting hand on Michel's shoulder.

I tried not to smile.

"But the real question . . . " said Alec primly, looking over at me.

"What is EES hiding?" Mei interrupted.

"What are they dumping?" said Ling.

"And how can we make use of the present crisis to better understand animal development?" said Ava.

"And save lives," said A.J.

"And write a paper," said Fenhua.

"Two papers," said Michel.

"Hundreds of lives!" said Mei.

"Three papers!" said Ava.

Could I possibly be prouder? Suppressing another sort of smile, I held up a hand.

When there was quiet—lab head's privilege—I began to outline three of my own models on the chalkboard. Lines and arrows and . . .

Ava eventually interposed. This was all very well, she said. But how were we going to *test* any of this? Didn't we still need . . . ?

Seconding this, Fenhua held up a collection tube.

"But no one is going to let us drive through there . . . " said Mei.

" . . . Certainly not with collection tubes," said Alec.

Excellent points! I acknowledged them. It was, however—since I had started—critically important that I finish outlining the third model on the chalkboard. So I did. Briefly. But as soon as I set down my chalk, I found myself, rather than listening, staring out over my students' heads, at the three portraits that paneled the back of the seminar room.

I had hung them myself.

The first was of Wilhelm Roux (a pair of spectacles + a mustache). The second was of Hans Spemann (also a mustache, but his eyebrows were much fiercer). Both had made seminal contributions to developmental biology.

The third was of John Snow (mutton chops). He had made a different kind of scientific contribution.

John Snow, 1813-1858.

(The students' joke, given my feelings for him, was that I was simultaneously too young and too old for him.

They were right about that, too.)

Something about this picture always got to me.

Suddenly self-conscious, I returned my attention to my students.

(Had they seen me staring?)

None too soon: the meeting was devolving alarmingly. Mei and Michel were now putting together some sort of militia. Ling was proposing a helicopter . . .

I held up my hand again.

"I have a rowboat," I said, when I had again enforced quiet.

After a few beats, Fenhua and A.J. laughed.

"They would kill you," said Mei.

"Don't!" begged Alec.

"John Snow would never forgive you if you died," said Ava.

(It seems they had seen me staring.)

"To the contrary," said Mei. She pressed a hand above her heart. "*Then* they could be together always."

The bell rang, 4 P.M. There are few things I am strict about. But the sanctity of my lab group's time has always been one of them. I have never held my students past the hour.

I wasn't about to make an exception today, not for the trivial purpose of defending myself.

Lab meeting over.

*

In fact, I *did* have a rowboat.

In another river, far away and half a lifetime ago, when I had been a field biologist, this boat had never let me down.

In the Y. River, though? Rowing against the current? Beneath searchlights? Some decades past my days as a field biologist?

I did—admittedly—just about die.

Even before I set off the security sirens.

What followed, I would later realize, was only a rain of tranquilizer darts. I was certainly lucky not to have been hit. But even if I *had* been I likely would have survived.

Probably?

Probably.

All the while, I thought about all the people who had already died.

I thought about John Snow.

I thought about the models—still untested—that I had outlined on the chalkboard.

I thought about my students.

Past the spotlights, the sirens, the darts, I at last reached the efflux pipe. Here, quickly, lifting and re-securing each cap, I filled three tubes directly from the pipe. Then, with an oar, I pushed off downstream.

Whoosh!

When I reached I distant section of the bank, I abandoned my boat (dear boat!) and my oars (dear oars!). Muddy and wet, I crashed through the forest until I reached the street.

Could I possibly sleep, after all that adrenalin?

Would John Snow?

Back at the lab, in the very early morning, I set a dropper's worth of efflux on a microscope slide and adjusted the magnification.

There, dark and wriggling, swarming and thick, with fatter heads and thinner tails and curved backs: a not-unexpected waste product, perhaps, from so comprehensive and productive an editorial enterprise as EES, and yet I had never seen so many . . .

Commas.

*

EES belonged to an industrial lobby, which retained a team of excellent lawyers. In a normal year, they would have gotten exactly what they wanted.

But there had been too many deaths that winter. This was not a normal year.

When I filed my report, a team was sent out to investigate. Afterwards—within days—an emergency desist order was imposed. Pending environmentalist reforms, EES would be shut down.

Let the industry lawyers protest that if they liked!

Of course (and this was something that the public and even many policy makers didn't understand), this order would have no immediate effect.

Affected bear embryos, once triggered to develop into killers, would not commit any violent acts until well after birth. So, even with the commas gone, multiple stopgap measures, including stricter firearm control, would likely be necessary for many years to come.

(Another urgently important question, which we would, of necessity, leave to other investigators: In a region of the world where such controls were already very strict, where were the animals even acquiring these weapons?)

Over the next many weeks, we performed new tests. To accelerate our experimental timetable (and to ensure that no destructive morphotypes would survive to maturity), we raised our test embryos in glass dishes, not inside of mothers.

To use this *in vitro* system, we took advantage of a proxy measurement that had been established in earlier studies: a marked difference in the level of a biomarker that could be detected very early in development.

Our results were unequivocal.

Under normal conditions—the sorts of conditions that (at least in a pre-industrial world) usually prevail in nature—an *Ailuropoda melanoleuca* embryo will nearly always develop into morphotype A: a panda that eats shoots and leaves.

But if commas, even at a fairly low concentration, are added to the *in vitro* nutrient solution (and the same, pending confirmation, is presumably also true when commas are introduced to the diets of pregnant *Ailuropoda melanoleuca* females), an embryo will often develop into morphotype B: a panda that eats, shoots, and leaves.

In the embryo, this difference seems small.

Everything about an embryo is.

But among adult pandas, present in the real world, it is catastrophic.

Morphotype A sits placidly amid the trees, chewing on strips of vegetation. Morphotype B seeks out human settlements. Here, in eateries of all varieties: corner cafes, neighborhood bakeries, 4-star restaurants, grocery store salad bars and gastropubs, it orders food. It enthusiastically consumes it. Then it pulls out a firearm. Blood spills and bodies heap: cashiers, waitstaff, chefs, and fellow customers, until the carnage has reached some sort of level that the panda seems to regard as sufficient.

At different stages in my career, I have reviewed the video footage of these incidents. But *that* is the point that I have always fixated on, the one where the animal makes that judgment: enough.

Again and again I return to that moment: rewind and replay, rewind and replay. As I watch, I try to determine—without ever being able to determine—*why* the animal decides that, just then: why it stops so abruptly.

Then it leaves.

*

That afternoon, our lab was celebrating. Our paper, "Differential Development in *Ailuropoda melanoleuca* Embryos Induced by Exogenous Punctuation Marks," had just been accepted by an excellent journal.

We had also received yet another commendation from an environmentalist organization.

In the "wake" of these achievements (aquatic pun intended! Ling and A.J. gleefully informed me), the students had commissioned a trophy for me.

It was intended, they said, to commemorate my nighttime journey along the Y. River.

They presented it to me over cake and champagne, which we shared at one of the lunch tables in the courtyard of the Biosciences Complex.

On the top of the trophy, a metal rowboat was mounted. "Bravery in Collection" had been inscribed beneath it.

I wiped my eyes ostentatiously.

"John Snow would be proud," said Michel.

"I think maybe John Snow would date you now," said Mei.

I lifted my glass.

It was two o'clock—a time for toasts. We took turns making them. Then Alec solemnly distributed slices of the cake, on which he had inked our paper's title, "Differential Development . . . ," in dark icing.

Delicious.

As we ate, Fenhua pointed to one of the courtyard food stands. Wouldn't—he reflected—this cake would pair excellently with "something savory"? Then he held out his hand.

I handed him the lab credit card.

"Something salty," Michel disputed, after Fenhua was already halfway across the courtyard. He put out his hand for the *second* lab credit card.

I handed it over.

There was no chalkboard in the Biosciences courtyard. (I had long regretted this.) So when, inevitably, the conversation turned to the diffusion rates of grammatical pollutants: parentheses, colons, semi-colons, apostrophes, and so on, at different temperatures, we were forced to make use of sketchpads.

Luckily, I was carrying several.

And when—also inevitably—the news turned to the latest (and deeply disheartening) environmental news, Ling began talking (and, at my urging, sketching) about gases.

"To gases!" said Michel, who had just returned to the table. Setting down his tray he had acquired, he lifted his glass, in which champagne bubbles (gases) sparkled: pop, pop, pop.

Wasn't this supposed to be a jolly occasion?

"*Aerosols,*" Ling clarified. Because, of course, following the crackdown on EES and the moratorium on river dumping, this was how some editorial companies had taken to disposing of their factory-based waste.

This was nothing worth toasting to.

Michel lowered his glass.

As we crunched on what Fenhua and Michel had just purchased, Ling expressed the outrage we all felt. How little sense this made! Airborne punctuation marks were even *more* dangerous than water-borne ones. In the air, they could get *everywhere*! There weren't—true—any laws against this yet, but . . .

"Laws!" sneered Ava.

I was about to echo this. But then I looked at the champagne, trophy, and cake on the table—and at Alec, who had made that cake and who was now looking at me mournfully—and I thought better of it.

This could wait until tomorrow.

"Well," I said, again lifting my glass. "We are lucky that pandas have such a restricted geographical range!"

Alec giggled uncomfortably at my morbid humor. Michel gave me a betrayed look: we hadn't toasted to "gases" but we would be toasting to this?

In the end, everyone *did* lift their glass, on the force of my authority, but no one's heart was in it.

Cheers.

Afterwards we sat in silence.

A.J. was staring at the cake. "Do you suppose," he asked suddenly, "that pandas are the *only* species that is sensitive to punctuation marks during their early development?"

"No one knows," said Mei curtly.

This possibility had, of course, been addressed in our paper's discussion section. Perhaps A.J. didn't remember. By adapting our *in vitro* system, it might, of course, be possible to test this. I had, however, long been unimpressed by the "fishing expedition" style of research; unless—I strongly felt—we were very clear on what we *might* be searching for, we risked wasting immense amounts of time and money. (And—in this case— embryos.)

On one of the sketchpads, I began to delineate this key point for A.J. and the other students: How important it was to maintain a *focused* line of inquiry. That our first priority should be . . .

Then I lost my train of thought.

Past A.J.'s head, I had caught sight of something.

A cluster of birds—perhaps 20—were pecking at the ground of the Biosciences Courtyard. Birds—true—were not my specialty, but it was immediately obvious to me that they were not native to this region.

I didn't even recognize the genus.

Perhaps they were resting, mid-migration.

Where had they come from, I wondered, in all that large world of sky?

(And what sort of pollutants had their mothers inhaled, when the eggs that would house their early development were first being synthesized?)

((Man eating pheasant./Man-eating pheasant.

Eat your chicken./Eat. Your chicken!

The colon: with her, sparrow is savage.))

At the same time, with growing unease, I noticed several things:

• a server from the food court, setting down an immense platter of sandwiches in front of these animals, directly beneath their beaks

• the awkward, constrained way that the animals hopped on and around the platter, as if they were concealing something bulky beneath their wings

• a certain quality to the way the animals cocked their heads (even as I knew very little about birds). An expression . . .

"We're leaving now," I said.

Ling stared at me, one savory snack suspended, halted mid-chew. Ava, reaching toward the second platter, was similarly frozen.

"It's time to get back to work," I said.

"But—" said Mei.

As I stood, I picked up both the trophy and the champagne.

"Alec, the cake," I nodded. Eyes wide, he lifted the box.

"And the trays?" said Fenhua.

"Now," I said.

They all got up, with different degrees of alacrity (jokes aside, wasn't I the boss?), and then I herded them before me.

I had studied hundreds of these cases. I knew what would happen if these animals were to sense that we knew.

If they were anything like pandas.

The courtyard was nearly full. In it, hundreds of scientists and university students were enjoying late lunches, or staging, like us, some afternoon celebration.

All of them.

I experienced a sudden and terrible temptation to shout my conviction, and to precipitate a stampede that would only make what was about to happen, happen faster.

And hinder our own escape.

Instead, I pushed my lab group past them all, all of the people, all of the tables.

In barely a minute, it *would* start. The violence here, and at many sites all over the world, over the months and years that followed, would be far more horrific than anything that any panda had ever been able to stage.

Pandas are solitary creatures.

But birds travel in flocks.

In just under half a minute, we would be inside the building, inside the brick walls that would turn out to provide an imperfect protection, inside a makeshift bunker paneled with the pictures of Roux, Spemann, and Snow.

But birds can fly. This maneuverability, combined with their greater numbers, would enable this flock, in this large food courtyard and in the Biosciences complex adjacent to it, to inflict 50 times the carnage that a morphotype B panda, acting alone, might have managed.

Still, because I was able to get my lab group inside, we would be spared the worst of it. We would only lose Ava.

And Michel . . .

Only?

But it could have been worse. And that, for years and years after, would provide a sort of comfort to me, even as it would provide no particular comfort to the families of Ava and Michel.

It could have been so much worse.

"Hurry," I said now. In my growing panic, I selected a word that was not at all nonchalant. And, in fact, the speed at which I was increasingly pushing them felt even less like nonchalance. Instead, it was desperate and jerky: the sort of motions that morphotype Bs were preternaturally predisposed to notice.

My rational brain knew that.

When I looked over my shoulder, I saw that one bird had already lifted its head from the platter. Its eyes were beady with an unnatural (but familiar) inclination, which industrial pollutants had shaped, inside the membranes of a clutch of eggs, somewhere. I saw its wings lift and the silvery flash of what lay beneath them. Those eyes . . .

Meeting mine.

I dropped everything: the trophy first, then the champagne. And when A.J. and Alec stopped abruptly in front of the puddles of champagne, in an apparent desire to clean them up (to clean them up??), I hissed, "Get inside! *Get inside!*" and when they wouldn't, I grabbed them by their elbows and I forced them forward, while the broken glass crunched beneath us. Because I had to get them out; I had to get all of us out . . .

Before the killing started.

The Anatomy of a Dream, Part 6
(Or: 4 More Reasons)

1. The duck-rabbit, first published in 1892, is your favorite optical illusion.

(Not that you particularly care for optical illusions.)

In a way, you do love it: beak-ears, nose-skull, feather-fur, cotton tail-wing.

In another way, you do not.

Is that a beak?, others wonder, delightedly reacting to the image. Or is it a pair of ears?

But when you reach for it, knuckles brushing against a smooth, flat surface . . .

(Or knocking persistently, Hello? Hello?, as if against a door . . .)

((Or smashing, as a magician might, against a faulty hat . . .))

You deeply resent the fact that it is a trick.

Is that a beak? Or is it a pair of ears?

Yes, you say fiercely, fundamentally rejecting the question.

Yes.

2. People used to feel things.

Didn't they?

But they don't now. Instead, everyone is numb. Everyone is isolated.

But if we were, instead, to mash two lives together—both human and animal—then meaning in that *one* life would be *doubled,* and the spiritual experience would be concomitantly intensified.

The feeling, also.

Feeling restored, by contact with another feeling. Feeling + feeling.

Feeling feeling.

3. It will not be possible to secure habitat sufficient for *every* endangered animal: the Bornean elephant, the white rhino, the

Arctic wolf, the leatherback turtle, the mountain gorilla (etc., etc., etc,). But if one were, instead, to compress the problem, and build elephant-rhino-wolf-turtle-gorillas (etc., etc., etc.), then a little of each species might be saved.

It's not the ideal solution—you acknowledge that.

But it is the only practical one.

4. You may have your detractors, but the Patrick Swayze that you do is really highly convincing.

You *are* him, in fact, in the moments before attachment.

(For whatever that is worth.)

But then you let go of that.

Then you become something more.

"Nobody puts the Great Pacific Octopus in the corner," you say.

You raise the creature to you in a spill of red. The surgical team you have commissioned begins the meticulous ministrations necessary to suture its tentacles to the muscles of your shoulders, arms, and fingers.

The needles bite into the numbed tissues; afterwards, as you and she (you-she: Great Patrick, Pacific Swayze, Octopus Man) begin to dance, saltwater burns against the stitches.

But it is a good kind of hurt.

Hybrid Shakespeare

Act 1.

Once there was a war on an enchanted island in the middle of the sea.

Or rather: there was to be.

Everyone wished to war with that island.

Oh, everyone.

The ships massed from Naples; the ships massed from Rome! The ships massed from Venice, Messina, and Pisa!

But the island was part of an archipelago—the youngest section, most recently emerged from the sea—and it was not allowed to go to war until the older islands did.

Act 2.

On the Senate steps, under the cover of this talk of war, a coterie of conspirators attempted to murder Caesar.

But Caesar had foreseen this.

When the circle parted and the bloody toga was lifted, the conspirators discovered that what lay beneath was not Caesar at all but rather two of Caesar's servants, R. and G.

(It was clear, at this point, that Caesar must have destroyed the original letter!)

Then R. leaped up, not dead. He explained that he had not been born in the usual way; his birth, to the contrary, had been assisted by a surgery, and he was therefore not subject to the usual laws that governed death.

But Brutus sneered. Was R. not aware that he, Brutus, had an identical twin—Cassius—whose blade had *also* skewered R., clean through? And that R., for this reason, had been twice-killed?

R. fell back down, again dead.

Enough tricks.

"To the islands!" Brutus snarled.

Act 3.

She was tamed, as an island only can be tamed, by being persuaded to confess to a series of absurdities: old is young, sun is moon.

She was tamed, as an island only can be tamed, by being humiliated in front of her family and friends on what was to be her wedding day, as the man who was to marry her instead accused her of infidelity and cast her off.

She was tamed, as an island only can be tamed, by being excoriated for her honesty and disowned by her father.

She was tamed, as an island only can be tamed, by being compelled to dress up like a man.

She was tamed, as an island only can be tamed, by waking up after a long sleep to discover that everything has gone quite wrong.

She was tamed, as an island only can be tamed, by falling in love with a man but being incapable of telling him because he believed that she was a man, while the entire time—and here was the real joke—the actor who was portraying her was actually a man.

She was tamed, as an island only can be tamed, by being exiled to a remote and magical section of the ocean, where a feral spirit attempted to assault her.

She was tamed, as an island only can be tamed, by being unable to remove the blood spots from her hands.

She was tamed, as an island only can be tamed, by not really being an island at all and by confirming the audience's belief that (outside the stylized thought experiment represented by this performance) islands don't belong on stage.

She was tamed, as an island only can be tamed, by being forced to witness the ritualistic sacrifice of her son.

She was tamed, as an island only can be tamed, by being assaulted and having her hands cut off and her tongue cut out.

She was tamed, as an island only can be tamed, by serving as a demonstration of the fact that the experience of being an island is most effectively conceptualized by a male playwright and most effectively brought to life by a male actor.

She was tamed, as an island only can be tamed, by being murdered.

Act 4.

At last—once most of the islands had been tamed—the war could proceed.

One side lost.

The other side won.

The losers poured poison into their mouths and poison into their ears. They set deadly snakes against their breasts. Then, when the snakes had bitten them and slithered away, they extended the fang marks with stabs from their daggers.

But the winners played viols, lutes, trumpets, drums and pipes. They ate dates and quinces and cake and good strawberries and wild boars roasted whole. With sack and ale they heated their livers. Then, in a garden, on a golden boat, in a besieged city, under the trees, they swore by the face of moon (for no vows are more constant) and made the same vow in wine (for no vows are truer) and then they carved it, for permanence, into the bodies of living trees (for no parchment is more sensible).

Act 5.

And then they got married.

A Brief Accounting of All of the Times I Thought I Was Pregnant But Later Turned Out Not to Be

1944.

I was only 4. But hadn't the Virgin Mary been scarcely more than a child?

And why wouldn't God choose me?

"What would you like for Christmas this year, Margaret?" they asked me.

"A baby!" I shouted, and patted my stomach expectantly.

1956.

I was 16. And I knew: This would not be God's baby.

This time, I would burn for it.

I would burn for it in Hell.

1957.

Turns out—more than what I had been doing with Liam was required to make babies!

So this time, really.

This time, for real, I would be roasted and disemboweled (and, hopefully, too—if there was to be any silver lining—rendered *not* pregnant, too.)

In Hell.

1958.

More than—turns out—what I'd been doing with Patrick, either.

But this time?

1961.

It had to be stomach flu! It really had to be stomach flu, because *he* was ralphing too.

I was so relieved!

Unless . . .

"Are *you* pregnant?" I asked him nervously.

1962.

All the confession, all the repentance.

I couldn't do it anymore.

(Could I?)

After rehearsal, in one of the rooms in the back, among the linens and the unconsecrated hosts, I told Sean, the choir director, that I was leaving.

I had always really liked Sean.

Really, really.

"Immaculate," I whispered.

1963.

At my next social group we did not eat Eucharist wafers. But rather: bean sprouts.

Instead of ceremonial garments, sanctified in a font in Rome, we wore tie-dyes and tights.

We did not pray. (Not exactly.)

Instead, during my first guided session, I looked deep inside myself. When I opened my eyes, I felt so *changed.*

A chakra baby?

"It happened!" I confided to the yoga instructor.

1964.

Just my appendix, actually. And they cut that out!

1965.

New friends, new rules.

"When the Xephrovs emerge from the lava beds," I said, "I hope that they will choose me as their vessel."

"They won't choose a woman," said Harvey contemptuously.

All the other men, dressed in the same red robes, gave me pitying looks.

Chauvinism . . . but without a Holy Mother Mary?

What was even the point of this group?

"We'll see," I said grimly. I patted my stomach even harder

than Harvey was now patting his. Then I set my gaze into an even more aggressive expression of transcendent expectation.

Choose me, Vulcan Underlords, I telegraphed telepathically.

March 1966.

The Peace Corps.

Wasn't I saving the world? Wasn't I helping?

"You're not supposed to have sex with the native men," my supervisor told me.

"Oh," I said.

May 1966.

Still the Peace Corps.

"Just with me," my supervisor explained.

"Oh?" I said.

1967.

I loved science. (Didn't I?)

Many primate species, Dr. Beverly explained, were at the brink of extinction,.

Humans—the notable exception—were also primates.

What she was proposing would, of course, only be an experiment. But theoretically? Given how similar the uteruses of all primates were?

From the freezer, she withdrew a frost-bitten vial.

"Save the lemurs!" I agreed.

1968.

"You are susceptible to cults," said my psychoanalyst.

"You're right," I said. Wasn't he always right?

And sideburned. And cheekboned.

And he had a couch.

1969.

After psychoanalysis—better than psychoanalysis—I discovered the Accursed Crystal of Akbradh-Neville.

Muriel Dolores, the Temple's priestess, urged me to look deep into the Crystal's interior. If I searched earnestly enough, she promised, I would "find Satan."

I squinted.

"And Satan's seed . . . "

I squinted harder. Emptying my mind, I tried to lose myself in the Crystal's facets, which were a deep, deep purple. Through these facets (was I starting to lose myself?), silver lines twisted, something like a labyrinth. Inside these lines, I tried to find . . .

" . . . Bam!" the priestess concluded.

And in fact, coincident with that "Bam!," I experienced a familiar jolt.

"Muriel Dolores," I asked, "will you be my friend?"

1970.

Save the whales?

1971.

I needed something real and important. But also a little magical.

Re-engineering history?

Perfect.

"We're severely understaffed," said the Time Council Recruiter. I noted, with a little shiver of excitement, just how quickly he was copying down the numbers on my identification documents.

Awesome!

Even better, though? He wasn't really *copying* them. Not with a pen, at least. Or even a Xerox machine . . .

What *was* that device?

So cool!

I really, really didn't want to ruin this. But I also thought it would be only fair to warn him.

"In a few months," I said. "I mean: what if, at some point"— here, I gestured down at myself—"I were to need to take some leave . . . ?"

"Fine," he said.

1541.

My first mission!

As my time ship skidded to a stop, conflicting feelings sloshed inside my stomach.

Fear. Excitement. Vertigo.

Something else?

Amelia, a pilot recruited from 1937, had already briefed me on the possibility of "tachyon tumors"—aggressive, particle-based growths, which (like a pregnancy) could sometimes take up residence inside of an inexperienced time traveler.

These "pregnancies," Amelia had explained, were especially awkward for male recruits. Then, laughing, she had gone on to relate a story about her navigator, Fred.

It was not a very reassuring story.

Oh, dear, I thought now, as my insides lurched.

Poor Fred. (Poor me?)

"I feel weird," I reported into my radio log. (My first entry!)

Then I threw up on the dashboard.

1798.

High school French. Why hadn't I paid closer attention in high school French?

"I read about you in school," I said, even though it was strictly forbidden to share anything so personal.

(Everyone at the Time Academy had been very clear about this.)

Stupid, stupid, stupid.

"What?" said Napoleon.

1806.

The Time Council had decided, after all, NOT to alter the course of the Napoleonic Wars.

Even though I had begged them.

It seemed impossible, at this point, that our son would rule France.

Napoleon didn't know why I was crying. I couldn't even *tell* Napoleon why I was crying.

Instead, pulling him close, I placed his hands above what I then believed to be the lump of our unborn child.

"Hold me," I said to him.

1997.

Just my gallbladder, actually. And they cut that out!

1703.

Let me eat cake, I thought.

At the Court of Versailles, the food was excellent.

Which was surely the reason for the weight gain.

And the nausea.

And the being 6 weeks late.

Could I get over Napoleon by eating more cake?

1935.

I knew that Dr. *Schrödinger* had a wife. And other women, too.

Critically, however, he was not Napoleon.

So I was with him anyway.

"I wonder," I began hesitantly, "I think that perhaps . . . "

Dr. Schrödinger looked up distractedly from his papers. With his pen, he dazedly traced the air. "But how will we know if it is a cat," he said, "until you give birth to it?"

Too rich for my blood.

"Erwin?" I said.

1200.

I was done with the Council. So done!

And I was done with men. So done!

(I'd also—for the time being—given up cake.)

But can you ever escape your past?

Even in the past?

In the nunnery, I tried to lose myself. When I failed, when my very dreams betrayed me, I confessed my struggles to Mother Beatrice, the Mother Superior.

"Dreams of physical desire?" she said.

I wailed.

"In defiance of your vow?" she said.

I fell to my knees.

"Dreams!" she thundered. Then she began, just so sternly, to explain that to dream was the same as to do. (Did I really not know that?) That, in every way that mattered, dreams of sin were equivalent to the sin itself.

(What a doomed, vile novitiate I was!)

As I wept at Mother Beatrice's feet, I wondered if, somehow, in the stink and the strangeness of this pre-technological evening, there might be some deep truth to what she was now insisting upon. If, by the rules of 1200, she might be right.

Not about the damnation part, really. But about . . .

I did the math on my fingers.

"Then I will give birth in October," I said.

2294.

Just pancreatic cancer, actually. And they cut that out!

2541.

Again and again the Time Council had tried—and failed—to go this far.

But wasn't I usually up for an adventure?

And wasn't the Council so determined to solve this problem that they were taking all volunteers?

At first, breaking through, I was SO excited.

But then I was attacked by . . . creatures.

With . . . tentacles.

With surgical equipment!

And they implanted something inside me.

[in transit]

I regained my ship! I time-jumped!

And the creatures (aliens?) did not follow!

(Did this mean they couldn't travel in time?

One could only hope!)

My implant pulsed painfully.

As if it were . . . feeding?

As if it wanted to come out.

2295.

Aliens!, I reported, when I reached the Time Council's Headquarters. In the 2500s, aliens ruled the earth!

To the Council, I presented:

• pictures of the Alien Kings, who had demanded my allegiance

• a map of the complex of cages (the size of a continent!) in which earthlings were held as slaves

• a recording of the sounds (was it music?) that had accompanied my brutal surgery

• the outline of the *thing* that the aliens had implanted

Lifting my shirt, I showed the Time Council exactly where.

"A tracking device!" the Council Head hissed, then immediately summoned a surgical team to remove it.

(I was grateful, yes. But also?

Ouch.)

When the implant was out of me (so bloody! still pulsing!) the Council Head herself destroyed it by setting it on fire.

Good old-fashioned, 23rd century fire.

Nothing beat fire.

(Did it?)

"Holy darn!" exclaimed Amelia when I emerged from the Time Council's chamber. "You look worse than Fred did! Remember that time"—and here she elbowed her navigator—"in the Pacific? When you developed tachyon tumors? When you were sick as a dog . . . "

"She looks fine," Fred interrupted.

"So do you," I said.

He was holding out a hand. But I didn't even take it. Instead, I only looked at him, he at me. Like we were mirrors. Strange—terrible—things had already happened to both of us: internal, psyche-rattling things, everything wrong.

We had so much in common.

Fred!

"So do you," I repeated.

1910.

We needed to destroy the aliens.

But not in the 2500s. That would be too late.

Instead, the Council decided, we needed to destroy them well before they ever left their native world and began their decades-long journey to earth.

The best way to destroy them?

(And not just them, but their entire solar system?)

A star virus!

Eleanor, a biochemical-astrophysicist who had been recruited in 2310, had already designed one.

But, until the virus reached that target star, it would require a human host.

"We'll have to heat you from the center out," Eleanor explained. "That's how stars do it."

I remembered the old question; I remembered the smiles of my grandparents and Sunday school teachers, while the Advent candles burned:

What would you like for Christmas this year, Margaret?

(The Star of Bethlehem!)

"Light me up," I said.

2417.

We'd messed up. More than a bit.

My injection, like many of the injections, had not taken. But others' had.

(Whoops!)

In human hosts, the virus had been packaged, then sent out in 1-person ships, aimed at the aliens' sun. Then, in fact, the virus *had* infected that sun. But having done that, it had gone on to infect many other suns as well.

Every sun, actually. And all of the space and matter between them.

These transfers had happened right away—faster than light.

(The physics of star viruses, Eleanor now ruefully explained to us, had turned out to be very different from the physics of light.

How unexpected!)

The aliens were destroyed. But now so was everything else.

Now—and in every When—Reality was fragmenting.

Only a few of us remained. Outside the Council's Headquarters, we could perceive just how close the End was. From the window, we could see the ground splintering, the sky splintering.

Everything splintering.

How soon we would all be Nothing!

There was only way to fix it now. We would have to go back to the very beginning.

A new Big Bang!

Only Eleanor, Amelia, the Council Head, and I were left, together with a few dear ones I had hurried to rescue, when the danger of the growing disorder had first become obvious.

Though what could "rescue" mean now?

So few of us . . . and almost no time.

While I had been out on my rescue missions, Eleanor had stolen an embryonic Universe from the year 2453—the height of human science, just before the aliens' arrival.

(Eleanor and I were resourceful in different ways.)

This embryo would require a human host. And Eleanor was the only person who would be able to administer the injection.

From a distance, from the control panel, Amelia would be needed to plot the coordinates for the human host's radical flight, to send that host and the seed back, far, far further back than any of us had ever been.

And I?

Yes.

I looked toward two of the people I had brought with me. The Council Head, Eleanor, and Amelia had insisted on keeping them locked in a glass room in the back, out of a concern (which—I had to admit—was pretty reasonable) that they might otherwise try to interfere.

(No one else knew about the third.)

They were reminders, all of them, of why this Universe was worth saving.

I took a breath.

When Eleanor implanted the seed, I felt the heat of it; it was the germ of a 100 billion trillion suns, of 100 billion trillion stories—everyone and everything.

It was inside me.

"Go!" shouted the Council Head.

But I did not go when Eleanor offered her hand, helping me up from the table. Not yet! Instead, I pivoted away and stumbled into the glass room in the back, so that, one last time . . .

"Kiss me," I said to Napoleon.

"Punish me," I said to Mother Beatrice.

And they did.

His lips. Her scourge. Together, *together*, and it wasn't—for once—even necessary to ask which I needed more, because—if only for an instant—I had them both; I had exactly what I needed, until they, like everything else, began to boil off into shadows.

(The third—still safe—was already in the transport vessel.)

I leaped back, just in time, into the main room, while the Council Head, beginning to fade, pushed me up the steps to the boarding platform of the transport vessel, then slammed the door behind me.

"Go!" cried Eleanor, as she too began to fade.

"Now!" cried Amelia.

Amelia was also fading. But, just before she went away entirely, she pressed a button on the control panel.

Lift off!

Absolute 0.

I am here in what used to be the Beginning.

It is the only place the virus has not touched—cannot touch.

Outside, it is empty and cold.

Everything depends on me, and what may or may not be inside of me: the germ of Everything writ very, very small.

That germ, succeeding.

Or failing.

The Promise: a whole Universe that will be, or won't.

And all I ever saw or almost saw (or ever thought of, or never thought of): Liam and Patrick and Amelia and Fred and Eleanor and the Council and Napoleon and Mother Beatrice and Earth and the aliens and the Milky Way and every visible star and the billions of galaxies beyond.

And the Virgin Mary.

I had been too afraid to seek Her out before.

"Mary," I say now, because I have found Her. After everything had begun to dissolve, I had gone to Her time and told Her that I needed Her.

She had come with me.

Now She is here, in the transport vessel.

She is here!

Her face is lined, the veins in Her hands are prominent, and She is radiantly beautiful.

She is listening.

"What was it like for You?" I say now, trying to capture it. "What was it like"—and here I gesture at myself—"the *waiting*?"

"I was never pregnant," She says.

Her smile is infinite and sad.

"You!" I say. I laugh and laugh and laugh; I laugh so hard it is like crying.

"That was only ever a story."

"Never pregnant!" I bluster. "*You*, the Mother of us all!"

"No," She says softly.

"A story . . . " I falter.

She nods.

"But Your Son . . . "

She shakes Her head.

I do not want to hear this. I do not want to know this. I do not want this clarified, whatever it is She means.

Not now.

"I need You," I say. I am holding Her hand; in mine, the bones of Her age-inflamed knuckles are like rosary beads. "I need You, I need You," I repeat, squeezing Her fingers. "When I give birth, I will *need* You."

"You are hurting me," She whispers.

I let go, yelping apologies: so sorry, so sorry, so sorry. She opens Her arms, and I fall to Her. She holds me, as if perhaps I am Her child.

And I am. Am I not?

I *am*.

In personal, subjective time, I have not slept for days and days. I have not . . .

Peace.

When I wake, She is sleeping too. Her arms are still around me—old and frail and beautiful.

I gently disentangle myself. I tiptoe past Her; I tiptoe past our stores of oxygen and food: more than enough for one, and just enough (for a while—for long enough) for two. I press myself against the transport vessel's viewing window.

I look at the emptiness, at the absolute nothingness, at the End-Beginning.

I look down at myself.

If I am—if it grows—Everything.

If I am not—if it does not grow—Nothing.

I look out again into the dark.

And I think that I feel . . . I think that, inside myself, I begin to feel.

Something.

The Anatomy of a Dream, Part 7 (Or: 3 More Reasons)

1. Many people make mistakes.
(Other people.)
You know this, because you are constantly observing them.
You are taking careful note of . . .
• each blunder of insufficient ambition
• each gaffe that proceeds from a vision that is not (let us be forthright) a vision at all but rather a pedestrian derivation of something that has already been made, done, imagined
• each . . .
(But you could fix these, if you were permitted to; you could swap out their tiny ambitions for your grand ones.)
((You wouldn't mind at all.))

2. Nature makes mistakes, too.
Mistakes of sequestration, separation.
Boundaries between species.
Boundaries between genera.
Boundaries between kingdoms.
(But you can fix those, too.)

3. Let me help you, Nature, you suggest.
Let me repair that.

Life Cycle
(Or: Why Stories Live Forever)

2.

On the appointed day—your "birthday"—you prick your finger on an antique spinning wheel. You do not cry. Instead, groggy and slow, you lower yourself quietly onto a mattress that has been set aside for this purpose, and you sleep, sleep, sleep.

3.

"Mother," you whisper.

A hundred years have passed. In that time, you have dreamed continuously: intense, flickering dreams, consisting of light and wind and green and earth.

Now, as you wake to the patter of rain, everything is different. Especially you.

In a riot of thorns, you cover the castle. You spiral around the watchtowers; you swarm over the rooftops. You descend into the moat (which, in your sleep, you have already drunk dry) and deep into the wine cellars.

You loop magnificently; you bristle impenetrably. In every archway, you are a door. In every window, you are a curtain.

But there is also something sad mixed in with the rest: a reminder, which, for a little longer, you will hold tight to, in that little attic room at the center of you.

(It is not Mother.)

Just you, just the husks of an earlier self.

Yellow skull and yellow hair, set upon a yellowed coverlet. A jumble of rib bones, just beside, where your central stem meets your central root; you cracked them long ago. Scraps from a lacy gown (the gown that Mother gave to you), now thin and crumbling and giving way to dust.

It hurts, growing up. It hurts, moving on.

That part always hurts.

4.

That spring, after waking, you begin to run.

You gather yourself to yourself: all of the sugars you have built with the assistance of light; all the nutrients, too, that you have taken from the soil, sourced from the bodies of the gardeners and the horses in the stable, whose sleep was triggered by your own, and from all of the palace servants, feasting guests, and the other members of the royal family.

("Mother," you whisper.)

Energized by what you have gathered, you race through the topsoil. Within weeks, you comprise a vast circle, many leagues in diameter. At the edges of this circle, at regular (but tastefully discrete) intervals, you erupt from the soil.

Your tips are fresh and green.

Wherever you emerge, you seek out elevated structures. Fences or bridges will serve. But walls are best: broad and high, ideally, and topped with firm, flat stones.

After choosing—after climbing—you perch.

From each of your many vantage points, the castle is a shadow, a barely perceptible bulge at the horizon; a faraway darkness.

Or rather: it would be. But your leaves (which are, in their own way, as sensitive as eyes) are not facing in that direction. Instead, you are reaching outwards, and you are no longer thinking about the past.

Not really.

Mother?

Mother is not here.

5.

In late spring, you bloom.

Your flowers are rugged and robust. They are also very large—approximately the size of a wine cask. Even more striking than the flowers' appearance is their smell.

Everyone is drawn to it.

Creatures of all kinds come to you—whatever happens to be native there, in the far-flung regions in which you now bloom, one flower per perch. They include:

A talking pig.

A gingerbread man, whom others cannot catch, but who seeks *you* out, on account of your scent, and who lingers briefly and voluntarily with you.

A pair of enchanted boots.

Billy goats, in series: small, medium, large.

A horde of rats pouring from a filthy city, led by the strains of a pipe. At first, they are driven primarily by music, but then they are driven primarily by you.

A courtier bearing a glass slipper on a satin pillow, house to house to house.

An ogre in its last hour, splintered and bleeding at the base of a beanstalk; an ogre who, after its fatal wounding, chooses to spend its last moments with you.

A flying carpet.

A fleet of animate brooms, determinedly conveying buckets up a hill, enlivened by the magic of a rogue apprentice.

A Papa Bear.

Asexual beings do not last for many generations.

So you ensure that, before departing, each of your visitors leaves something with you—a bit of themselves:

A narrative outline.

Sperm or pollen.

A bundle of pages composing half of a story.

The novelty that you acquire at this stage will be critical for the continued survival of your kind.

Sometimes, testicular scissors and testicular syringes, stored at the base of your petals, assist you in this acquisition.

In other cases, you do not need them.

Whatever you take, you fuse with the inheritance scripts that already compose you. Inside yourself—stirring and reassembling; compiling and commingling—you construct experimental variations on what has already been a very successful theme.

(You.)

6.

In the summer, each of your flowers becomes a fruit.

Each fruit is large and bright. Along the vertical axis, its colors are symmetrical. In each case, the effect—very crudely—is something like a human face.

The purpose of each "face" is theater.

"An egg!" shouts the first of many observers: a peasant in a lane, carrying sticks on his back; a baker selling pies on a wheel-drawn cart; a child leading her lamb to school. "An egg on a wall!"

7.

All summer, crowds gather around you, ever larger.

When the wind blows, sections of your husk vibrate to create a spectrum of sounds.

Humpt tie. Dumpt tee.

Harp-toe. Deemp-tweed.

Exactly *which* sounds emerge is influenced by the seeds that quiver inside of you—clusters of immature future yous.

These differences, in turn, reflect the unique nature of the seeds' paternities.

As a result, these sounds differ from fruit to fruit, from perch to perch, from region to region.

Humpat Jeetiedoo Tuey.

Ha' M'dumpi.

In some regions, you seem to blubber like a baby. In others, you make rhymes. You mimic animals. You sing. You speak nonsense syllables in a raspy voice. You hum and murmur and shriek.

Humpty Dumpty.

Hûmpé Dûmté.

All sounds, no words. But at each of your fruits, people come to watch and listen (even as you listen to them). In low voices, they debate among themselves. By turns, they come to decide that you are . . .

. . . a mystic

. . . something adorable: a baby form that will one day mature into a pet or a village mascot

. . . a whisperer of secrets . . . delicious secrets

. . . the ghost of someone beloved, briefly returned to earth, to say . . . what?

. . . a god

As the summer wears on, members of the crowd come to emotionally depend upon you. Every day, they need you ever more profoundly.

(As you, in a different way, will soon need them.)

At the same time, your stem is becoming weaker.

. . . ever weaker . . .

Then it snaps!

From your many perches, at many moments (which are, in each case, precisely synchronized with local conditions), you tumble down.

Sometimes, someone in your adoring crowd will catch you. Usually, though, you elude them, slipping instead to the ground.

But even when someone *does* catch you, you still shatter.

It is important that you shatter.

8.

Your interior, yellow and viscous, percolates among your admirers' boots, sandals, and bare toes.

The crowds weep and scream.

For them, your end is an outrage that it would be unwise to argue with, a tragedy that, for those who do not already understand it, it would be impossible to explain.

Reverently and frenetically, they collect the pieces of your shattered husks and attempt, again and again, to fit them together. When they fail, they petition their governments.

If you are not—they threaten—reassembled?

Violence in the streets!

If you are not resurrected?

Rebellion!

Where rulers—emperors, sultans, kings, dukes, counts and so on—are wise, they take their subjects' concerns very seriously. They outfit lavish delegations, manned by their personal servants. Each is tasked with restoring you.

But the tiny, quivering germs of you that were once contained in the fruits' husks—the only parts that really matter—were not, in fact, harmed by the husks' shattering.

They were set free!

Long before the servants arrive (riding quadrupeds of different kinds: camels, horses, zebras, and burros, depending on the region), these germs scurry into cracks in the ground. They—you—quiver in the shadows in the grass.

As the royal delegations assemble, you remain hidden. As the servants and their steeds lose themselves in the intricate puzzle of the husks' repair, you wait.

Soon, though, some of these yous begin to exhale a potent signal. To the royal servants and their steeds, this signal is imperceptible. But to the other tiny, quivering yous, it smells like . . .

Scout! Mobilize!

. . . Surround all the horses . . .

. . . Surround all the men . . .

. . . Surround all the watchers . . .

As the signal passes through the air, and as more of you receive of it (more and more!) and as more of you respond, first by releasing more of the signal (more and more!), and then by swarming . . .

Your signal shifts.

What you release (now, now, now!) is even more potent and even more urgent, and to all of the yous that receive it (now, now, now!), it smells like . . .

Attack!

Attack!

Attack!

Parts of you are very sharp. These parts are tipped with poison.

The people and steeds that you have *not* poisoned observe with concern the collapse of those that you *have*. As they bend to inspect the fallen, they too are easy to poison.

If any outside creature—not you—were to preserve memories of these moments, they might end up telling the wrong story. That, in the long term, would make this harder.

Happily, though, you are tiny and quick. Though some survivors (almost none) and witnesses (nearly so few) do attempt to run, you are able to hunt most of them down.

(Mother . . . you think.)

Your poison is deadly. But it is also useful for dissolving dirt and loam. By exuding more of it, you are able to dig deep, broad pits.

Into these hollows, scurrying back and forth, you transfer all of the remaining flesh and accouterments of the members of the delegations.

Good meat—the meat of royal servants!

Good cloth—the cloth of royal servants!

Good tools—the tools of royal servants!

You have always had a taste for the best. You have always, when you can get them, preferred articles that are fine and costly.

(Mother . . . you think.)

You gird these pits with rock, which will hide and protect you.

Then you are still.

9.

Your transformation is risky and slow.

Certain yous, encased in some of these underground hollows, will be destroyed by rot or soil insects. Others (more rarely) will be killed by some canny relative of the human dead, who correctly interprets a clue you did not intend to leave.

But there are so many of you now, many thousands, each of them stemming from that original, castle-centered you.

Some survive.

The bodies of your would-be rescuers nourish and enclose the surviving yous, like . . .

(Mother? you wonder foggily.

No.)

They are—rather—raw material. Delicious and massive and visceral, they supply you with everything that you will need to fundamentally re-create yourself, inside and out.

So, although all the King's horses and all the King's men do not, in fact, succeed in putting you "together again," they do, in the end, accomplish something far more important.

They fuel your metamorphosis.

10.

As you transform, you diverge into three morphological types: the Ones who Hunt, the Ones who Enclose, and the Ones who Wait.

Once they—you—are mature, these three types dig their way out.

As a One who Hunts, your head is shrouded by a brilliant red covering. It is colored like (and in part literally with) the blood of the humans and ungulates you have eaten.

This covering—a hood—conceals the part of your head where hair would be, if you had any.

But this form is only temporary and hair is expensive to make. Hair is not necessary.

An additional frill of red tissue, extending from your neck, covers the rest of you, all but the face.

At a different stage in your cycle, you engaged in puppet theater. Not this time. *This* face is detailed. It is, to all appearances, human, juvenile, and feminine.

(Mother?, you think.)

As a One who Hunts, you scout through forests. (If you are forced, moors or scrubland will also serve; so—under certain circumstances—will a prairie or a desert.) You know exactly what you are looking for.

(Not Mother.)

A wolf!

Perhaps you do not have hair. But the parts of you that receive and interpret scents are very well developed and very, very keen.

All the better to smell them.

When you find a wolf (or other large carnivore), you replicate the language that you learned when, as a fruit, you immersed yourself in the locals' speech.

Like the parts of you that receive and interpret scents, the parts of you that make sound are versatile and adept.

"I am going . . . " you explain to the wolf (or other large carnivore). "I am going to . . . "

The wolf attends greedily to the directions that you go on to provide: instructions for reaching the two other kinds of metamorphosed you.

As the One who Hunts continues to scout for more wolves (more, at every stage is better than one), a second variant of you becomes visible to the wolf that hurries towards it.

The One who Encloses.

As a One who Encloses, you resemble a building, untidy and hodgepodge. It is the apparent dwelling of someone very poor.

In you, the one-time possessions of the Men and their Horses: their saddles and swords and armor and egg-mending tools, have been digested and repurposed, so that you resemble . . .

A cottage.

All the better to conceal.

Inside is the frame of what ostensibly appears to be a bed, together with the faintest, slapdash suggestion of additional furniture.

The other furniture is not necessary.

The One who Encloses also contains your third and most important morphological variant:

The One who Waits.

As the One who Waits, you consist mainly of a wrinkled head— again no hair—topped by what appears to be a nightcap. This head is attached to what appears to be a blanket and what appears to be a nightgown, which is attached to a tube of edible meat.

All the better to infect.

It is not in the nature of wolves to notice such irregularities. (Although, admittedly, in some areas, in proportion to your own success, the frequency of these once less-usual wolves is increasing.

But you too are adaptable.)

And once the One who Hunts has first suggested that enduring story: the timelessly compelling narrative of the waiting grandmother, tasty and feeble, your wolf is particularly unlikely to notice.

Instead, it feasts.

Only later, once it begins to feel very thirsty, may your wolf begin to suspect something. Perhaps, by the time it begins to experience this thirst, it will have already appropriated the garments of the One who Waits, in confident expectation of a second course that will never arrive.

Perhaps not.

But, as the need becomes violent, the wolf will leap off the slapdash structure that is not really a bed. It will rush howling out of the One who Encloses and into the forest.

The wolf's thirst is powerful. But it is also strangely specific. In the throes of it, the wolf may lope past many apparent—but fundamentally unacceptable—sources of relief: dew on leaves, farmers' watering troughs, moist earth, gutter runoff, muddy ditches, puddles of rainwater.

Instead, your wolf holds out for a body of water with very particular properties: moderately sized, freshwater, and with many outgoing streams.

All the better to assist your dispersal.

"Water!" it howls, splashing into the lake, lagoon, loch, reservoir, or basin it has chosen, before dog-paddling frenziedly toward the center of it. "Water!" it burbles, even when its mouth and its stomach are full, and when its pelt, too, is very, very wet, and the weight of this liquid, both inside and out, pulls it down and down and down.

11.

Your wolf is dead.

Inside it, and inside the decaying bodies of many other wolves across distant regions, you are present in the form of generative sacs, surrounded by soft shells.

Eggs.

(Sort of.)

Within these sacs you grow, nourished by the musky mixture of molecules that arise when wolves (or other carnivores) rot. When you are large enough, you hatch out, then eat many paths through the wolf's rotting flesh—many thousands of you per corpse.

Tadpoles.

(Sort of.)

Heads thrashing, tails whipping, you swim down rushing rivers or trickling creeks. You drift through many outlets, wide or narrow.

At a remove from this wolf—and all the wolves—from which you have hatched, you disperse in all directions.

In that tower room, far away and long ago, you were one. But now you are many: prolific and legion, proliferating and everywhere.

At once you are one story, diverse and multi-faceted. But you are also many stories.

You are too much to follow all at once.

So, as a narrative device (narratives, often enough, are amenable to these; narratives—as has been repeatedly documented—are disposed to thrive on them), we will follow only one.

Because all stories, at their heart, are the same.

Or at least they aspire to be.

So, let us trace only one, from this point forward.

One tadpole.

12.

The pond that you discover is perfect. It is set in a sun-dappled grove, framed with elegant trees.

You decide that you will settle here. You will take your gamble here.

Your resolution is both profound and irreversible. At the trigger of it, your limb nubs extend and your tail recedes.

You become a frog.

(But not just any frog.)

((When have you ever been just anything?))

Instead, you are a frog who adores shiny objects.

In the pond you have chosen, you follow every shimmer and every glint. You pursue the shadows of what might be . . . what could just so possibly be? . . . a silver spinning top or a sapphire gaming set or an emerald pogo stick or a diamond hula hoop or a ruby stacking block, clumsily wielded, then permitted— Splash!—to fall.

Usually, of course, such a flash will be nothing: a pebble, a snowflake, a scale-mailed fish.

But, whenever you find such a shimmer, you hunt it down. Because it *might* be a toy. And when it is, *when it is!*, you will dive in after and you will retrieve it. With it, you will leap pantingly from the water to the bank and return it to the well-propertied youngster to whom it belongs.

The vast majority of your tadpole siblings will never encounter such a child. But, in the end, in order to make the cycle work, only a few of you need to.

You are one of them.

Your story—this particular you—turns out to be *the* story, out of many stories, the story to which all stories aspire.

You are the archetype.

*

One spring morning, you chase a golden ball through the water, down to the pond's muddy bottom.

Kicking back up, swift and strong, you return it to her. To *her*. To a girl in ribbons and silk . . .

This girl . . . ? Surely, this girl . . . ?

Surely!

When the child runs away (privileging her disgust for you over the loss of her treasure), you become even more certain.

You go after her, hop, hop, hop. The ball is heavy, but you persevere through the strain of it. You trail her, slowly but surely. You watch as, far ahead of you, she passes over a drawbridge and up the steps and into a building that is immense and venerable and ancient and crenelated . . .

. . . a castle!

Yes!

Across the drawbridge, you also go, hop, hop, hop, then up the grand staircase. At the top, you throw yourself persistently against the castle door, thud-splat, thud-splat, thud-splat, until an astonished footman lets you—and the ball—inside.

"A frog!" say the servants who tumble in from the kitchen.

"The princess' ball!" says the maid in the hall.

Two servants are sent upstairs, the first tasked with coaxing the girl from her bedchamber and the second with summoning the Queen. A third is sent to the throne room, where the King now confers with his advisors.

It is a potent story, the Frog Prince story. Even if it is not exactly your story.

Soon, the child comes down the stairs, holding the Queen's hand.

Kiss him.

Kiss him.

The servants have taken up the chant.

The girl is whispering fiercely to the Queen. She doesn't want to touch you!, she says. She never wants to be near you!

Kiss him.

Kiss him.

At the bottom of the stairs, the King bends to whisper into the child's ear: That a princess, when she can, should please her people. That traditions are important.

Kiss him!

Kiss him!

The footman sets you carefully on the girl's palm. In her eyes, as the chanting intensifies, you see the same question.

This frog prince story . . .

Is it your story?

The transference granules are ready. They coat your mouth, your tongue.

Transmission is almost assured.

Closer . . .

Kiss.

"It's dead!" the princess screams. She flings away the final husk of you. It collides—thud!—with the stone wall, then splats to the floor.

The chanting ends abruptly. Laughter replaces it.

The maid laughs as she sweeps up the body, preparing it for a "state burial" in the garden rubbish heap. The butler laughs as he retrieves the golden bauble, then directs the scullery boy to remove the slime of its "sovereign aura." Even the Queen laughs, just a little, as her weeping daughter buries her small face in her skirt.

"It seems he was not a prince after all," the King says.

And maybe you weren't.

Maybe, depending on how these sorts of things are calculated, you were not royal before that kiss.

But now you are.

1.

You begin in her mouth. But that is not where you stay.

You burrow into her throat, then her stomach, then her blood. You infiltrate her bones, her skin, her brain. Down her nerves you pass, branching and branching. Then you take her heart.

Soon, there is no more her.

Everyone is so good to you!

They play with you: jacks and cards and puzzles and clapping games and running games and swimming games.

You are a natural swimmer!

You adore talking; you chatter nonstop about wind and rain and leaves and sun. (And they listen to you, though you are not—they think—a ghost or a prophet. They listen!)

They comb and braid your hair. (You have hair now!)

They give you air, water, and food. But they also give you love, which is rather like but also unlike (and better than) many other things, including:

- performing for a crowd far below
- using scissors to harvest inheritance scripts
- giving directions—and flesh—to a hungry wolf

But even better than love (even as it is bound up in love; even as it is *exactly* what love is) is the fact that *she* is here.

Mother!

She is different from before, from any time before. Her accent is different from any Mother you ever had before. Her face is different; her language and her clothes are different.

But she is also the same.

Mother pushes you on the swing in the garden. Mother gives you presents. Mother reads to you, whenever you ask. Mother tells you about her own childhood, in a kingdom far away. After the maids prepare you for bed, Mother kisses you goodnight.

When you say, "Mother, look at me!" Mother looks at you.

Every year, Mother works with the royal dressmakers to prepare a new gown for you, a birthday gown.

Every year, that gown is larger!

In more time, somewhat after your first menses, something else in you begins to enlarge: a fibrous bundle with incipient root hairs. You can feel it when you press upon yourself.

Your finger begins to itch.

In the attic, at the top of the castle, you create a room that is just for you. (This is the prerogative of a princess.) You furnish it instinctively, like a nesting animal: a goose down mattress, a spinning wheel.

Your finger itches.

You dream. Sometimes, when you sleep, you feel as if you are falling, then shattering on the ground. (Or feasting, neck deep in blood.)

As weeks pass, these dreams becomes more intense.

Sometimes, before you wake up, you cry out, and Mother—not the maid—rushes down the hall in order to attend to you.

Mother is a light sleeper.

One night, one difficult night, the night before your birthday, she comes to you again. When you open your eyes, words in your throat, you see that Mother is staring at you.

It is not quite as before.

"That song," she says, after a long moment. "Where did you learn that song?"

You try to smile.

But Mother does not smile back. In the candlelight, her expression is . . . what?

You have seen that kind of look before, sort of; sometimes you catch her eyes on you like that, sidelong.

But this feels like something more.

You swallow.

"When I was a girl," Mother says, "my brothers disappeared in the service of an errand—a silly, futile errand!—and they never came back."

That is very sad, you say.

"That song you were singing just now," she says, "What was it?"

You say you don't know.

"But where did it come from?" she asks.

You say you learned it from the maid.

Mother says that seems unlikely.

You say you remember now. The gardener was humming it. She should ask the gardener.

Mother says that is a lie.

Your mouth opens. Closes.

Mother says that, before her brothers disappeared, Mother even went to see it: the Magic Egg on a wall. Mother says the Egg was singing the song that you were singing just now! That it sang and it sang and it sang it!

You stare at her.

"Where did you learn that song?!"

"The cook," you whisper.

Then Mother is very close to you; her arms are tight around you. It is almost like an embrace. But it is also a violent search—what the palace guards might do to a prisoner.

"Don't!" you say, with an adolescent's wounded dignity. But Mother finds it anyway. She finds it, though you try to twist away: the slight, not-quite-human nub that protrudes from the bottom of your rib cage, the one that has only recently become perceptible—the tip of a vegetative coil. Even the servants who assist you in your dressing have not noticed it.

You have always been so careful.

"You are a Changeling," Mother says.

You push away her hands.

"There weren't even any bodies," she says. "I didn't even get to say goodbye!"

You try to shove her. But your great sleep is near, and you are not very strong.

"Changeling!"

She is holding your arms. You can no longer move them. At the same time, you are dimly aware that she is removing something small and jeweled from her nightdress. Something . . .

It is, you realize, her dagger—the sort of dagger that all royal women carry. A weapon of self protection.

Yours is in your dressing table, on the other side of the room. Too far.

"Ever since that frog!" Mother says. You sense the dagger lifting, a blur above you. You feel her arms stiffen. "Ever since that ball!"

You struggle . . .

But it is no use. You are moving so slowly.

So instead you look away from the dagger. Instead, you look at her.

You force her eyes to meet your eyes, the way you cannot force her arms.

"I am your daughter," you say firmly.

Your eyes are bright and clear, the same as ever.

She stares at you. Into you.

Have they ever been different, your eyes?

Then Mother lets the dagger fall. It thuds harmlessly onto the edge of the bed, then onto the floor.

Mother says that she is sorry.

She hugs you, weeping. You hug her back. As you lie together, you subtly adjust one of the pillows between you, so that she will not again, by accident or intention, touch the nub that is already protruding from you.

You can both pretend that it is not there.

Mother says that she loves you.

Tomorrow is your birthday. Tomorrow, you will put on the birthday gown that Mother is preparing for you: the perfect one, the one that, for weeks, she has been whispering about with the dressmaker. Tomorrow, you will prick your finger. At the trigger of it, your own sleep will begin. As you sleep, you will release clouds of persuasive potions, which will induce everyone in the castle to immure themselves in the garden. There they will all lie, waiting to serve as nutrients once your roots extend that far.

Your finger itches.

"I love you, Mother," you say.

You hold her and are held by her. Mother's flesh, as you snuggle against it, is still soft and immediate. You embrace her with your arms, not your root hairs.

For a little longer.

And you are not a vast being, immortal and always, preparing for an additional act of propagation: to ramify everywhere; to colonize new landscapes; to infiltrate new hamlets, villages, cities, and futures; to imprint yourself in new memories, new dreams, new hearts.

That is for tomorrow.

On a shelf beside your bed, there is a well-worn book. You reach for it now. When you hold it out to her, you give her a smile, a smile from your heart, the smile of a child who is far younger than you even externally seem to be. When Mother takes it from you, it falls open to a well-worn page.

Your favorite chapter.

"Tell me a story," you say.

The Anatomy of a Dream, Part 8 (Or: 6 More Reasons)

1. Bacon is delicious. Steak is delicious. So sometimes you imagine what it would be like if these two tastes, two textures were instead compressed into a single animal and into a single cut of meat.

(Not sometimes.)

((There is in fact, a part of you (stomach-brain-heart-mouth) that is always . . .

. . . considering . . .

. . . ruminating . . .

. . . wistfully salivating.))

But it isn't on the menu.

(Is it?

No.

You open it to see.

No.)

So you pen it in anyway, in a font that (almost) matches the rest.

Then, beneath your breath, you order it.

Baak, you mumble. Stecon.

What? they say.

But they heard you.

Where it matters (stomach-brain-heart-mouth), they heard you.

((You cannot have that, they say; you cannot have that: this abomination that we have no inkling of, because we did not hear you.))

As you mouth fills, ever moister in misplaced anticipation, you continue to speak through the liquid.

Baak! Stecon . . .

(What?)

gurgle

Baak . . . Stecon!

((*What?*))

But they heard you.

Where it mattered, they heard you.

And then they said no.

2. You have observed the way that other people behave with their romantic partners. How they want to get their hands all over them. How earnestly they aspire to make their romantic partner *better.*

You do not have a romantic partner.

But you do have Nature.

3. Sacred cows.

Never touched, never challenged, never changed?

Well.

Well.

You will begin by taking them away, far away, from their protected enclaves, incensed altars, and diamond-festooned cages.

Then—reverently, ceremonially, irrevocably—you will herd them into a single breeding pen:

MOo!

(touch)

mOO!

(challenge)

MoO!

(change)

Once you have bred all these cows, merging them into a single genetic being, you will mash *that* with a zebra and *that* with an elephant and *that* with a sea serpent.

MooBray!

(reverently)

MooBrayTrumpet!

(ceremonially)

MooBrayTrumpetHiss!

(irrevocably)

4. Soaring trees, lovely flowers, and wild quadrupeds, gracefully grazing.

Some people would call this scene "majestic."

You, however, do not feel what others profess to feel.

Couldn't there be better? you wonder in response.

Couldn't it be more?

5. You go to the zoo every weekend. But not because you love it. You go, rather, because it makes you angry. And wistful.

(And a better, third, mashed-together feeling: a hybrid of the other two.

Angtful.

Wingry.)

After each visit, you fill out one of the comments cards that they provide to you, How was your visit?

How . . . ?

(So nice of them to ask!)

In your stomach, an enhanced feeling (angry wistful sarcasm) gurgles sloshes burns.

Clicking your pen, you answer their question with more questions.

Why don't the giraffes have fins? you write.

The butterflies tusks?

The penguins flagella?

Each time, you alter your handwriting and sign with a different pseudonym, in order to make it appear as if you are part of a much larger movement.

But they never do anything.

6. Nature, to a modern person, is something that is perceived from behind glass.

Like a museum exhibit.

This disconnect is so severe that it will likely require aggressive action to correct. Like . . .

. . . the surgical attachment of elk horns to the human skull. Like . . .

. . . a bit of muscles, from a frog or a sparrow, grafted beneath the skin.

Like, like, like . . .

. . . something inside, anyway (woodpecker hearts), something intimate (Komodo dragon hearts) something beating (dolphin hearts).

Can one, in any case, have too many hearts?

Men I Have Given a Fish

"What do you think?" I asked him.

He smiled wanly. Then, leaning forward, he sniffed the plate that I had so carefully prepared.

"It kind of smells like fish," he admitted.

*

He had enjoyed our date to the Aquarium. So, for our one-week anniversary, I wanted to go big.

I descended into the Mariana Trench. There, in the grotto of the Sea Witch, I secured for him dominion over all the fish in the ocean.

In exchange for my soul.

Later, as we stood together on the pier, I showed him how to flutter his fingers so that, in an expression of deference, a thousand fish would erupt from the water at once.

He certainly was surprised.

"Does this include the dolphins?" he asked at last.

"No," I said.

"Oh," he said wistfully.

*

After my diagnosis, I gave him a call.

"I have salmon," I told him. "You probably have it too."

"Salmon . . . ?" he said.

Over the phone, I could almost hear him unzipping his khakis.

And—with a curse—confirming it.

"It's not curable," I said. "But with medication . . . "

"Salmon?!" he repeated.

*

"You would starve if you didn't have me!" I said.

"I set the table," he said defensively.

"You *sat down* at the table!" I said. "That's different!"

"English," he said, and shook his head, playing up his accent because he knew exactly the effect it would have on me.

Inimitable l's, beautifully exotic vowels.

And again I was lost.

"More fish?" I said, and my voice cracked a little.

*

"Bones!" he cried, spitting out the first bite.

My eyes filled with tears.

"Many animals have bones," I tried to explain, after I had taken a breath. "Even humans."

"Maybe *you* do," he said.

*

I fought for him. Across the galaxy, from one of the great dark pools where time went slow, I drew forth an ichthyous beast. When I cudgeled it, its brains spewed, bright against black.

"I have conquered," I said, laying the great corpse at his feet.

"Ah," he said.

"From its bones," I continued, "we will build our marriage be—"

His eyes skittered away. Then I suddenly perceived it: an immense pair of caribou antlers, freshly mounted over the fireplace.

Another suitor's gift.

"I'm sort of with Kathleen now," he said.

*

"It's got eyes," he said uncertainly. "And it's looking at me."

As if he wasn't used to that.

So gorgeous.

"Look back," I whispered.

*

"I brought you something extra," I said to my accountant, interrupting what appeared to be a lunch meeting with another client. Leaning across his desk, I passed him the still-warm bundle.

Our hands brushed.

"It's trout," I whispered.

He smiled . . . and explained he was allergic.

Then he introduced me to his boyfriend.

*

His diet consisted mainly of Soylent.

When I set the cod bake in front of him, his eyes got very big.

"That seems, um . . . nice?" he said uneasily. "But if you want me to eat that, I'm going to need you to liquefy it."

Then he looked back at his phone.

*

I tied him up.

I teased him with a fillet of tilapia, first bringing it close and then moving it away.

"Give me!" he said, writhing delightedly. "Give me!"

His—admittedly gratifying—excitement aside, none of this was actually my favorite.

(I was ruminating, in any case, with growing warmth, on the pair of freeze-dried swordfish I kept in the nightstand.)

"My turn," I said later, poking him lightly.

But he was already snoring.

*

One evening, after a bass dinner, his eyes strayed out my window.

"Would it be . . . acceptable?" he said. "That is: if—ahem!—you were to show me where, in the pond outside, you've deposited your eggs, might you"—and here he coughed—"permit me to ejaculate on them?"

What?

"*I'm* not a fish," I said finally.

"Oh," he said.

*

He scarfed down his plate of marlin. He even asked for seconds.

But he never called.

And he never answered mine.

One evening, though, I glimpsed him through the window of a Burger King.

"Fins are fun," he admitted, after I ran inside to confront him. "But in the long term . . . ?"

He shrugged.

Then he took another bite of his cheeseburger.

*

Blue eyes, dark stubble.

I often did him favors.

Lately, though, things had gotten out of hand.

Outside the museum, I peeled off my ski mask. Then, unzipping my jacket, I withdrew the ancient fish fossil he had requested, *Primoquaticus urgenitus*.

It was worth millions.

"I'm probably going to prison for this," I said.

"I'll visit you," he said.

"Will you?" I asked.

In the distance, police sirens wailed.

"Maybe," he said.

*

Nothing ever lasted. So, as we walked together along the pier, hand in hand, I was already feeling doomed.

But then, spraypainted on the sidewalk, I caught sight of the old adage, "Give a man . . ." and it suddenly occurred to me:

Had I been going about this all wrong?

"Would you like to go fishing?" I blurted.

"I've never—" he said.

"I have a second pole," I told him, gesturing toward my skiff, which bobbed at the end of the dock. "I can . . . teach you."

He stared at me.

Nice eyes.

"I'd like that," he said, and smiled.

And I wondered, that smile.

If this time, maybe.

If.

The Time-Traveling Healer

I came—I enrolled—because suffering moves my heart. Wherever it is. Whenever.

Doctors without Temporal Borders.

In its service, I go to places in the deep past, places that lack the advantages, both conceptual and technological, that my education confers.

The portals through which we pass are in the Pacific, on a series of islands which barely emerge from the water and which were some of the last to be marked by any cartographer.

This archipelago is, as they say—or would have said, in another time (my traveling, I confess, sometimes affects my speech, and I find myself using quaint phrases)—at the "edge of the World."

It is certainly at the edge of Time.

How do these portals work? And why is it that, on these tiny islands, and within the networks of caves that twist beneath them, we can only set out in one direction—the past? And that, on our return journey, we are capable of traveling no farther than the point of our departure? That, in effect, there exists an entire category of destinations—the what *will* be—that we have never been able to reach?

It is curious.

But I am a healer (another quaint phrase!), heart and soul. I am a doctor, through and through. That is my identity and my only official qualification. And, though I do engage in occasional armchair speculation (though armchairs, in the Whens I am posted, are rarely provided to me), I will, in the end, leave these great Whys to other minds.

I am not a philosopher.

Anyway—and after all—it is the past that needs us.

All those yesterdays.

In previous postings, I was assigned to the Hundred Years War and to the Crusades. Here, I honed my bedside manner. I also discovered that the past is like nothing so much as a foreign country. Wherever one's When—whenever one's Where—culturally-specific arguments must be applied to overcome the patients' resistance to your unfamiliar methods. You must *persuade* them to allow you to heal them.

In spite of themselves.

My latest posting, however, is not merely in the deep past, but in the deep, deep past—3,000 years back, before historical and intellectual benchmarks that make the mind reel a little.

Before almost everything that we would regard as modern.

Before even Latin, the language of physiology and medicine, the source of long lists of imposing anatomical words: Brachialis, Ulna, Clavicula, and so on, that every medical student must memorize.

Before even Hippocrates, that Doctor of Antiquity, whose oath (and how fitting!) our time-traveling cadre has in part adopted.

Not born yet.

"You are abundantly qualified," said Dr. Harvey, one of the administrators of our organization, when he appeared to me at my last posting, disguised as an injured soldier from the House of Valois, in order to describe my next assignment. "You *can* do this."

"I can do this," I repeated. Because . . . couldn't I?

Can't I?

I have knowledge. And I have heart.

As for the rest . . .

"Stop!" I say now (the local now).

A band of four is crouching above a sick man. I think that they have good intentions (Aren't intentions so often good?)

But their tools!

I do a quick inventory. I see fire, a container of water, and a basket of withered leaves.

I do not recognize the leaves. And water (I suppose) can do no harm?

But I shudder to think what they hope to accomplish with the fire.

As if fire were some "god," whose beneficence might assist them.

Don't get me started; if I start, I will never stop.

None of the languages that I presently know—not even Latin!—will of course be of any use to me. ("That will be part of the challenge!" said Dr. Harvey, part in warning and part in encouragement.) So I follow my—to them—meaningless sound, "Stop!" with a series of emphatic gestures.

Halt!

No!

And they do stop; they stare back at me. Whether because of my volume or because of my gestures. Or—more likely!—in deference to the "miracles" that I shared with them yesterday: demonstrations of the cunning items I carry in my coat, objects that can bend light and generate sound.

They already have a sense of what I can do.

As I step slowly closer, I begin to mime what is wrong with this man—a thing which, even from a distance, even from the beginning, had been all too tragically obvious.

"Too much!" I say with an accompanying gesture. Expansion, superfluity. "Too swollen!" I say.

Not that they understand this either. But this time the problem is more profound than language.

To them, the body is not what it is to me. To them, it is— yes—an assemblage of liquids. But these liquids are not ordered according to any coherent philosophy. To them, the body is a place where "gods" war.

Don't get me started; if I start, I will never stop.

To save this man—and I have known this from the beginning!—I will have to take over.

"Stand aside," I tell them, keeping my voice kind, my gestures authoritative.

They do not move.

In what follows, I know well, diplomacy will be as important as medicine.

Slowly, I withdraw an object again from my coat. It is one of the same ones I used during my first demonstration at my arrival on the local yesterday. It is the one, in my judgment, that most impressed the larger group of which they were assuredly a part.

It is—quaintly enough!—the simplest of my objects. It has no intricate knobs or complex inner workings.

With it—just as before—I cause the glitter of the fire to glitter back at them.

They are riveted.

Then, through careful gestures, I communicate to them: I will give them this item, this mediator of the light trick, but they must step back.

I will give it to them . . . but they must step back

Way back.

"Farther," I say emphatically, even after the main negotiations have concluded, and I have given them their reward.

As they move away, I wistfully reflect that it *would* be nice to have an assistant. In a few months, perhaps, when my status among these people has grown and I am better able to communicate with them, I will begin to train one. I already have an eye on one of the boys.

But it is too early for that now.

This patient's case is too dire. My course of action is too clear.

I cannot risk anyone interfering or objecting.

And *my* tools? Ha!

At this critical stage of my early relationship with them (light tricks aside!), they would find these too disturbing.

When the band of four are far enough away, performing the light trick at another fire—a distant-enough fire—I block their view of what I am doing with my back.

My patient, lost in his own suffering, gives me a glassy look. When I make my first incision, he manages only a soft moan.

"Faster," I whisper. "*Faster.*"

My bowl fills.

When I have taken what I judge to be enough blood, I bandage the salutary cuts I have made. I use tested and true bandages, which have served patients in several other time periods.

Good, experienced bandages.

I do not know if this man will live.

I have rarely seen a patient whose humors were so severely out of alignment.

I have never seen a body that contained such an unhealthy excess of blood.

But I am giving him a chance.

It is the sort of chance that he never would have had if I had not come.

I shudder a little. And it is this shivery feeling, this inimitable mixture of gratitude and sadness, which no other experience has ever been able even remotely to evoke, that has long kept me in this service.

What would have happened to this man if I had not come?

When I have settled him in a comfortable sleeping position—when my bloodletting instruments are clean—I return him to the supervision of his people.

Tomorrow, I indicate to them, as best I can.

I will come again tomorrow.

At sunset, I retreat to my own tent. I stare into my own fire. Then, as on many nights in other Whens, I whisper the name of my homeland. It is not a message; this invocation serves exclusively an emotional purpose. For as intensely as I serve, I am still often desperately sick for home. It is a land that I must mark in numbers and not by place, in years since the birth of Our Savior (who, in this When, is not yet born). Anno Domini, and blessed be His name—

1642.

Harem

I had warned him: If he followed me, I would be his only wife.

Arkkh! he said.

Anguished.

But he followed me. When he did, he left all of his wives, his vast harem of elephant seal females, behind on the rocks.

On his body was hewn a tangle of proud marks: a record of his battles with rival (but lesser) males; a bloody price paid—and paid again—for the acquisition of so many consorts.

Scars.

But he left them.

Because I was worth it.

With a great roar, we ascended in my sky ship. Up into the wind, *Whoosh!*, we flew, then far past the atmosphere.

In a cabin of my ship, beside the receding light of his sun (first a fat yellow orb, then a glistening drop—like rain—then a pinprick, swallowed by the dark), we consummated what we had promised: mine and yours blurring to mours and yine (and myo and ineurs) and all one.

His wife.

As we entangled, I gave him another gift: immortality. From my own heart, I pulled a bright thread, which I pressed into his.

Immortal, my husband. Like me. Forever and ever, our bodies would remain like this, and death would never part us.

Because wasn't he worth it, too?

Arkkh, he acknowledged.

Yes.

As we continued into the dark, sky fires burned around us: the beginning of something eternal.

All these stars, my husband, and we would outlast them.

Arkkh.

We continued through these fires, then far, far past them, to a place where the light of his own sun would never reach.

Then we descended.

In his own land, he had been a lord and collector. But he was here now and he was mine now. Immortality tinged his eyes now, and it tinged the rest of him too. His scars, which were also mine, were luminous with it.

As we went down in the ship's elevator, then disembarked, I saw myself in him: reflections of reflections, eyes within eyes; he seeing me seeing him, again and again; me in him and him in me.

Husband.

From the ship's hangar, I led him into my palace of ice and glass, which was translucent and scintillating and blindingly diamond-white.

Did it remind him, this glitter, of his homeland?

Did it please him?

Arkkh.

And didn't that please me?

At the end of the final hall, I showed his quarters: an immense room of textured silk (and what eye could see to the end of it?), vast, vast, vast—if not infinite yet.

But I was working on it.

When I opened the door, the rest tumbled forward, clamoring in a—if not quite endless, then certainly near-endless—number of tongues, even as I, with an authoritative gesture, held them back:

A rooster with an extensive coxcomb: forehead to spine, which he had once employed in the subjugation of many hens.

An invertebrate lord from the planet Nandor, bristling with a helmet of phallic antennae—just decorative now. With them, he had once defended—and enforced—the possession of a harem of 10,000 wives.

A tentacled Duke of Glox, who had once possessed a harem of 2 million.

An Emperor of the Galaxy's Edge, former husband to more than a quintillion dancing particles, all the grains of sand, on all the beaches in all the planets in his realm and their every moon. He had, paradoxically, known the names of all of those consorts, even as he had been incapable of numbering them.

And others and others and others.

But none of their harems had been as large as mine.

"Meet your brother-husband," I said in my colossal voice, voice enough to fill the room, voice enough to silence them.

They were still.

"Meet your brother-husbands," I said more softly. This voice was just for him, the husband at my side: the newest, the dearest, and, for the moment, the freshest in my heart.

Arkhh? he said. His tone was strained and hurt. And in the room-wide stillness it was a very small sound.

"What did you think?" I asked him, not ungently.

Arkhh? he repeated.

It was the sort of question that they sometimes asked.

"My love!" I laughed, for my ship was humming. I could hear it in the hangar, vibrating with an updated purpose: a new proposal and a new target, in a galaxy far away. Into my earpiece, cracklingly, via my link with the ship's computer, the details were whispered: exactly where, exactly when.

In the ship's cabin: fresh sheets.

Arkhh?

Enough.

"I am going," I said.

But I gave him an encouraging nod. With it, I urged him toward his brother-husbands, toward my collection of collectors—toward the sort of domestic arrangement that was, to each of them, both familiar yet also not familiar.

When he turned again to me, hesitant, I gave him another nod—still more encouraging—for it seemed possible, if not inevitable, as it always did, that if not exactly yet, if not exactly now, that he would come eventually to realize—

How much they had in common.

One final caress; my dear, my dear. And, as I exited the door, pulling back for the last time, for now (even forever, even immortality, divided by so many consorts, is not, in the end, so very much), he gave me, more intense now, and now entirely wordless, a *look*. And, though he would give me many such looks in the forever and ever, it was sweetest now, most poignant and most touching now, when it was new. This first time.

That look.
Be still, my heart.
"Perhaps," I suggested, "you can talk about me."

Once Upon an Armageddon

"I'll huff and I'll puff and I'll blow your house in!" cried War.

Exhaling, War toppled a cottage of straw and a cottage of wood and a house made of candy and a witch's tower, which contained no door at all, only a single window. And an ensorceled castle covered in brambles, so that all its inhabitants died, crushed by the falling stones, without ever waking.

And the hill that Jack and Jill attempted to go up, but were instead flattened by. And a cottage-sized shoe. And all the rows in a pretty garden, which smashed in a confusion of tinkling bells, splintering shells, and terrified screams. And a castle in the clouds. And a clock striking 12. And London Bridge. And a great royal wall supporting a great royal egg, so that every part: stones, mortar, shell, and yolk, was shattered into fragments and hopelessly jumbled.

And once everything, everywhere, had fallen, and there remained not a structure on earth that deviated in the least from the horizontal, War loped forward, claws clicking in the rubble, and began to devour the scraps.

*

"You are just right!" cried Famine.

Spoonful after spoonful, she gobbled up the porridge of the three bears, ensuring that they would have no breakfast.

Opening her mouth still wider, she emptied a whole meadow full of clover, on both sides of the bridge, so that all of the Billy Goat Brothers, even the largest, dwindled, becoming small and skeletal. And the entire pantry of Jack Sprat and his wife (both the fat and the lean) and the pantry of another Jack, who, after selling his cow, became too weak and emaciated to ascend the beanstalk (which, in any case, Famine had already eaten).

And the curds and whey of Little Miss Muffet, so that, when the spider sat down beside her, the malnourished girl was scarcely conscious, and experienced no fear at all, only a nihilistic tiredness. And all the remaining vegetation, everywhere, so that the boy who had once cried wolf now instead whispered piteously to himself, "so hungry . . . so hungry . . . so hungry . . ." and Old MacDonald lost his farm, with a starvation event here and a starvation event there, EIEIO.

After Famine had stuffed herself, she became very sleepy. So she prepared a pillow out of a gaggle of emaciated bird corpses—a certain Goosey Loosey, Ducky Lucky, and so on, who had died as a result of her depredations. Their bodies were all feathers and bone, but no flesh. This made them soft, but not too soft.

Then, settling comfortably beneath a quilt composed of emptied grain sacks, Famine fell fast asleep.

*

"I am the fairest of them all!" cried Pestilence. But the Mirror did not agree. Instead, it returned to her a flickering series of faces: youths and maids and lords and ladies, all of whom—allegedly—were fairer than she.

Truly?

Pestilence shook back her sleeves.

Her fingers crackled. From her throne, she sent her lightning out. Through the sky it streaked, crackling over mountains and seas, until it struck a princess with hair like midnight and skin like snow, and a princess with golden hair, which fell in flowing waves, as long as summer. And a lovely peasant in a room full of straw and another in a pumpkin coach. And a charming prince. And a vain prince. And all the king's beautiful horses and all the king's beautiful men. And a dashing cat, impeccably dressed in hip-high boots. And a dainty man, fresh from the oven, whose perfect flesh was composed of gingerbread.

Where the lightning touched their vaunted faces, lesions erupted. A terrible fever coursed through their heads, burning their brains to cinders; another passed across their skin, inflicting deep scars. Their limbs fell off and their noses did too, and through the pits that remained they sneezed bloodily.

Pestilence shook down her sleeves. This time, turning back to the Mirror, she simply raised an eyebrow.

"You are," the Mirror affirmed.

*

"Who will help me make the sky fall?" asked Death.

No one would, of course—no one ever helped Death—and so Death reached up sadly, with a beleaguered sigh, and proceeded to do it herself.

She pecked industriously. As she pecked, everything fell: sun and moon and the enterprising cow that was suspended above the moon, mid-jump, and the twinkling, twinkling little stars, about which generations of children had wistfully wondered (massive, was the answer: lethal and hot), and all the layers of nighttime darkness that lay behind them. As the pieces crashed to earth, they crushed her, and they crushed War and Famine and Pestilence, and they obliterated, too, all the wreckage of the world, until all was still, silently ever after.

ABOUT THE AUTHOR

Rachel Rodman completed a Ph.D. in Biochemistry. At the University of Oregon, she has taught interdisciplinary science courses with titles like "Writing the Genome," "Matter and Impermanence," and "Evolution through Art and Story." One of her major research interests is "literary populations"—groups of related stories authored by different writers. In a literary population, 3-20 writers work in parallel, modifying, combining, and building off of one another's work.

Much of Rodman's fiction is conceived as an "experiment." Starting, for example, from an existing story, one or more characteristics can be changed, i.e., inverted, exaggerated, eliminated, or replaced with something new. The result is a "mutant" story. Characteristics from two or more stories can, similarly, be combined to generate a "hybrid." *Mutants and Hybrids* is a collection of 27 such experiments; you can read more at www.rachelrodman.com.

PRIOR PUBLICATION INFORMATION

- "The Wizard of Zo": *Asymmetry* (© 2019)
- "Jonah and Delilah": previously unpublished
- "It Really Is All About You": *Kaleidotrope* (© 2023)
- "Experimental Breeds: Bears, Clothed in Rumpled Hoods, Pipe 'Rapunzel' to the Sleeping Pigs": *PANK* (© 2011)
- "The Anatomy of a Dream": *E·ratio* (© 2019)
- "His Name-O": *On the Premises* (© 2016)
- "Do I?": *Etherea* (© 2022)
- "Snow White and the Seven Biblical Floods": *Sein und Werden* (© 2021)
- "The Evolutionary Alice": *Analog* (© 2020); reprinted in *The Lorelei Signal* (2023)
- "Seventh Date": *Dream of Shadows* (© 2022)
- "The Princess and the Pond": previously unpublished
- "Cures for Hiccups": *Daily Science Fiction* (© 2022)
- "Our Entire Relationship is Ironic": *Manqué* (© 2019)
- "Hybrid Bible": *Exist Otherwise* (© 2023)
- "Rock, Paper, Scissors": *Trembling with Fear* (© 2019)
- "Three Pigs, One Wish": *Zooscape* (© 2019), under the title "Good, Better, Best"
- "Hamlet in Midsummer": previously unpublished
- "4 and 20 Dead Cats": *Chrome Baby* (© 2022)
- "Strip Poker": *L'Esprit Literary Review* (© 2023)
- "The Comma: With Her, Bear Is Savage": *Kaleidotrope* (© 2023)
- "Hybrid Shakespeare": previously unpublished
- "A Brief Accounting of All of the Times I Thought I Was Pregnant But Later Turned Out Not to Be": *Electric Spec* (© 2022)